"THANKS ISN'T MUCH OF A WORD . . ."

Vicky's eyes met his. "But maybe I can find something better," she said. Slowly, her arms encircled his neck and she pulled his face down to hers, pressing her lips hard against his.

"Is this being grateful?" he asked.

She opened her lips in response, feeling his tongue probe their sweet softness. Fargo sank down on the grass, pulling her with him, his hand reaching into the neck of her blouse, pressing against one saucy breast.

"Oh, Fargo," she gasped, wriggling out of the blouse. Freed, her breasts curved upward, the nipples taut, quivering in eagerness as he bent down and sucked one hard little tip into his mouth. Vicky half-screamed and pressed forward, her hand at the top of her skirt, pushing the garment until it fell away . . .

Exciting Westerns by Jon Sharpe

THE TRAILSMAN
26

WARPAINT
RIFLES

by

Jon Sharpe

A SIGNET BOOK

NEW AMERICAN LIBRARY

PUBLISHER'S NOTE

This novel is a work of fiction. Names, characters, places, and incidents either are the product of the author's imagination or are used fictitiously, and any resemblance to actual persons, living or dead, events, or locales is entirely coincidental.

The first chapter of this book previously appeared in *Maverick Maiden*, the twenty-fifth volume of this series.

SIGNET TRADEMARK REG. U.S. PAT. OFF. AND FOREIGN COUNTRIES
REGISTERED TRADEMARK—MARCA REGISTRADA
HECHO EN CHICAGO, U.S.A.

SIGNET, SIGNET CLASSIC, MENTOR, PLUME, MERIDIAN AND NAL BOOKS
are published by The New American Library, Inc.,
1633 Broadway, New York, New York 10019

First Printing, February, 1984

1 2 3 4 5 6 7 8 9

PRINTED IN THE UNITED STATES OF AMERICA

The Trailsman

Beginnings . . . they bend the tree and they mark the man. Skye Fargo was born when he was eighteen. Terror was his midwife, vengeance his first cry. Killing spawned Skye Fargo, ruthless, cold-blooded murder. Out of the acrid smoke of gunpowder still hanging in the air, he rose, cried out a promise never forgotten.

The Trailsman, they began to call him, all across the West: searcher, scout, hunter, the man who could see where others only looked, his skills for hire but not his soul, the man who lived each day to the fullest, yet trailed each tomorrow. Skye Fargo, the Trailsman, the seeker who could take the wildness of a land and the wanting of a woman and make them his own.

*South Dakota, 1860, north of the Cheyenne River
and east of the Black Hills, a tinderbox
land where savage fury could erupt at any time. . . .*

1

Even the moon seemed to be waiting.

Almost full, it made the land a place of silver and long shadows. It hung low, as if watching and waiting for hunter and hunted. The leaves of the tanbark oaks hung unmoving, unstirred in the still air. The night creatures stayed motionless. It was a waiting night.

The big man with the lake-blue eyes crouched beside the Ovaro, hardly breathing as he waited. A hundred yards down the hillside, unseen now in the night brush, the others waited. Ten. Big, bronzed, near-naked bodies. Ten Crow bucks. And Skye Fargo's lips drew into a thin line as he asked himself the question again: why did they wait? Why had they come here to the top of this valley in the night to wait?

His eyes narrowed as he thought back but a few hours earlier. He had picked up the ten Indians as he'd ridden north after he'd crossed the Cheyenne River. He'd spotted them in time to take cover, stay behind and out of sight, a matter of simple self-protection at first. Crow, he had noted, tall, proud, even insolent, each sitting his horse as though he were a king. Two wore wrist gauntlets with Crow markings. And he had seen something else, warpaint on faces and chests. He continued to stay back but followed, and he had begun to frown. They rode almost in a direct line and two Conestoga wagons came into view. They paused only to look down on them and then rode on, and Fargo remembered how his frown had grown deeper. A little later, they saw two women in a buckboard, but once again the Crow only paused and rode on.

A war party that passed up two perfectly good chances to strike. It was out of character. It didn't fit the pattern of small war parties. Curiosity made him follow, and as the dusk began to turn the last of the day into purple grayness, his frown grew still deeper. The Crow didn't turn back. They continued their purposeful way, falling into single-file formation. He watched the night lower itself over the land, and the Crow continued on. One more strange, out-of-character piece of behavior, he'd noted. Like most Indians, Crow didn't like night attacks unless there was some dire need. Especially for small war parties. Yet these kept the ponies moving on through the night. Fargo followed, being careful to stay back far enough. The almost-full moon rose to let him see the column of silent riders ahead of him.

He stayed tailing them, curiosity still a part of it but there was more now. They were no idle riders out for a moonlit canter. They spelled terror, death, destruction. They wore warpaint and they had a target, someplace, somewhere, and suddenly lives were in his hands. He could spell the difference between survival and slaughter. And so he'd continued to trail the war party, hanging back under the pale moon, and he followed them into a lush valley. Halfway down, he saw them halt, slide from their ponies, and settle down. He dismounted, led the Ovaro a little closer, near enough to see that the Crow had settled down to wait, not to sleep. He moved a little closer and halted. Any farther and they'd smell him. He settled himself against a big tanbark oak, peered down into the valley, but the night let him see but a few dozen yards beyond the waiting Crow where he saw only oak and tall underbrush. He leaned his head back against the tree and the night stayed still, a waiting night.

His mouth turned down in displeasure. This was not how he had planned to spend the night, not for damn sure, he grunted inwardly. He had intended to be in Prairie Dog at this hour, in a real bed with a warm-fleshed woman. He let thoughts go back over the past forty-eight hours. He had run into a celebration when he brought the five big Owensboro California rack-bed wagons into Dustyville, each loaded down with everything from dry goods to whiskey. Dustyville lay just east of the Black Hills and damn few supply wagons were willing to risk the journey through the Sioux country and fewer made it. So his arrival with the wagons had become an instant celebration, a roaring, whiskey-flowing welcome. He'd enjoyed all of it, and it was still going on when he pulled out in the morning to head north and cross the Cheyenne to Prairie Dog.

His lips turned up, formed a smile made of anticipation. Dolly was in Prairie Dog and she'd be making him welcome once she got over being surprised. Dolly had written him months back to tell him he'd be welcome anytime, and to urge him to find a way to visit. The five wagons to Dustyville had given him a way and he smiled as he thought back of Dolly Westin and past years, let himself enjoy the warmth of good memories. But he snapped off remembering as he saw how far down the sky the moon had traveled. It would be dawn in another hour, he frowned, and still the Crow waited, deep shadows unmoving in the fading moonlight. Slowly, the last of the night gave way to the faint gray flow of dawn, and Fargo watched the grayness take on streaks of pink, as though the sun were reluctant to come out. He half-rose as the new day let the valley take shape and he saw the Indians stir, begin to rise. Fargo felt his mouth become a thin, hard line as, at the bottom of the small valley, he saw the three cabins.

He stared down the slope as the Indians began to move. Three cabins, three families trying to build a life in this untamed land, pioneers who counted on their own strengths to prevail over the savagery of nature and of the red man. They had built their cabins in a loose triangle for defense, Fargo saw, each cabin able to protect the other, and now he saw why the Crow had waited. They would let those in the cabins wake, come outside to fetch water from the well, stretch, greet the new day, bring in firewood for the morning coffeepot. The arrows would whistle through the air then, cut down those already outside, whether it be man, woman, or child. Others would rush out, pulled by love, care, need—emotions, not reason, governing their reactions—and another volley of arrows would find their mark. The full attack would erupt then, but the battle would be already half-won.

He understood their waiting now, their tactics, but little else. Why these cabins? Why had they passed up easier victories? The questions remained and Fargo drew the big Sharps from its saddle holster. The Crow were on the move, flying down the slope, pulling their ponies after them. They'd be in firing range in moments and Fargo quickened his pace, found a boulder, and slid to a halt. The Crow were still unaware of him, their attention focused on the three cabins. Fargo raised the rifle, saw the door of the nearest cabin start to open. The Crow froze in position, arrows on drawn bowstrings. Fargo fired, the rifle exploding the dawn stillness. Fargo saw the cabin door slam shut as one of the Crow buckled in two, pitched face-forward to roll down the slope.

Fargo dropped flat as the Crow snapped around, sought him, but they turned back to the cabins. They had committed themselves to the attack and they would follow through. That was their way, even though their plans had been shattered. Fargo saw them change from stealth to fury as they swung onto their horses, raced down the slope with their screaming war cries. But he saw the rifle barrels being poked through firing holes in the cabins, exploding in gunfire, pulling back to reload. The Crow fell back on their usual tactics, racing around the three cabins while pouring arrows into them. But the three cabins in their triangle managed to return a respectable volume of cross fire, Fargo saw as he pulled himself onto the Ovaro and started to move across the slope. He reined up to aim at one fiercely riding buck, fired, and the Crow flew from his horse, seemed to hang suspended in midair as the horse charged on, dropped lifelessly in front of the center cabin.

Fargo half-turned as he heard the crash of glass from the cabin to the right and saw four arrows cave in the small window. The circling Crow poured another hail of arrows at once through the smashed window, and Fargo turned his horse to head down the slope toward the cabins and the circling attackers. He fired the big Sharps as he streaked downward, saw a Crow catapult from his horse and saw still another take two bullets fired from the cabins and drop from his horse as though he were a sack of grain. The remaining Crow suddenly broke off the attack, veered away, and started up the slope. One made only a few yards before a shot from one of the cabins brought him down.

Fargo reined up as he saw the five Crow racing toward him, focusing their rage and frustration on him now, all too aware that without his warning shot they'd have had their victory. Fargo spun the Ovaro around and started up the slope, saw the Crow veer off in two groups to flank him, two on one side, three on the other. Their tough, short-legged Indian ponies made for the steep slope, he saw they were moving too close too fast. They'd have him outflanked in moments, to pour arrows at him from both sides. He could bring down some, but the arrows from the other side were certain to get him. He slowed the pinto, let the Crow come up abreast of him on both flanks, bowstrings drawn, when he reined up sharply and saw the first volley of arrows from both sides whistle past in front of his horse's head. He slid back across the Ovaro's rump and hit the ground, the Sharps still in one hand.

The Crow wheeled, started toward him again from both sides. He fired lying almost prone, sent the first buck flying off his pony with his upper chest caved in. The other four reined up, wheeled as Fargo fired again and another buck gave a strangled gasp, fell from his steed with one hip dangling as though he were a doll improperly put together. Fargo rolled, slid into deeper brush as he saw the remaining three Crow leap from their ponies and disappear into the high brush. He cursed in silent rage that he hadn't been able to bring down at least one more. They were more dangerous in the high brush, and he slid his way backward down the slope, halted, listened. The brush rustled above him, in a line with him and again to his right. He stayed motionless, ears straining, smiled grimly as he caught the sound of the brush at his left.

They were moving at him from three sides, the front and both sides. Once again, they were coming in to outflank him, this time with a pincer move from the front added on. And again he'd not be able to stay in place, and get the three of them at once. He waited, listened to the brush move as they drew in. They were crawling on their bellies, staying down beneath the top line of the high brush. The one coming down from above was moving the fastest. Fargo's lips pursed as thoughts raced through his mind. They expected him to slide downhill, give way before them. The two flankers would be moving downhill to anticipate that, he knew. He glanced down along his body, drew his leg up, dug his heel into the earth, dug it in again, and dislodged a clod of earth and small stones. He pushed with his foot, sent the stones tumbling down the slope through the brush. The stones clattered their way, simulating the sound he might make sliding downhill. But he didn't slide after them. Instead, he pulled himself up the slope, the sound of the stones covering his movements. He pulled again, the Sharps in one hand. He stopped, heard the Indian just above and in front of him hurry his pace, lift himself to his hands and knees to do so.

Fargo was there, waiting, as the astonished Crow came through the brush, the Indian's jaw dropping open as he saw the man he didn't expect to see. The Crow never closed his jaw as Fargo fired the rifle at point-blank range. His head disappeared, simply vanished, to leave the haze of droplets tinted red that rose up from the headless body. Fargo whirled, heard the other two Crow changing direction in the brush. They were scurrying away and he watched the brush move, saw them hurrying to their horses. He turned, raised the Sharps, zeroed in on the one to his left. But the Crow stayed low till he was around the far side of his horse, and then he vaulted onto the animal's back and lay almost flat across the horse's loins and withers as he raced away. Fargo's shot singed the Indian's long, black hair but nothing more, and he turned, saw the other Crow already galloping his pony up the slope. They had had enough and headed for a safer place.

Fargo waited till the sound of their horses was swallowed up in the new morning, rose, retrieved the Ovaro, and slowly started to walk down the slope toward the cabins. He'd reached the bottom when the cabin doors opened, the men coming out first, the women close after them, and the kids hanging in the open doorways, lots of kids, he noted as his glance swept the three cabins. A tall man with sideburns and a long face came toward him, hand outstretched. "We owe you, mister, all of us," he said. "Your shot saved us."

Another man, reddish hair and beard, came up. "Sneakin' savages, waitin' to bushwhack us afore our eyes was half-open," he said.

"They had it planned out, all right," Fargo said. "When a Crow rides, he rides well; when he shoots, he shoots well; and when he bushwhacks, he does it right, the most surprise for the least resistance."

"I'm Seth Hawkins," the tall man with the sideburns said. "This here is Jed Cranepool." He gestured to a third man, shorter with a young, open

16

face, who had come up. "Hiram Graney," he introduced. "And who might you be, mister?" he asked.

"Fargo ... Skye Fargo. Some folks call me the Trailsman," the big man with the lake-blue eyes answered.

Seth Hawkins nodded, his eyes taking on new respect as well as gratitude. "Heard your name back Kansas way," he said. "Those murderin' savages must've been waiting through the night for us to come out. How'd you spot them?"

"Been tailing them since north of the Cheyenne," Fargo said. "When I saw them pass up two Conestogas and a pair of women in a buckboard, I figured they had something bigger in mind." His eyes moved over the three men and their wives, who had come up to listen. "Any reason why they'd come here and single out you folks?"

"Hell, no," Seth Hawkins said. "Guess they don't need any special reason except to wipe us out."

Fargo's lips pursed. "These came special. There was a reason beyond that," he said.

"Such as?" the settler asked.

"Don't know and can't figure it out," Fargo said. "But there was a reason. The Conestogas and the two women weren't enough for them. They wanted you."

The three men shrugged, but the younger one, Hiram Graney, frowned in thought. "Things have been real quiet until the last few weeks. A trapper passing through told me to be careful, said there'd been three attacks. Something's got the Indians stirred up, he said." Hiram Graney's frown deepened. "But it's got nothing to do with us. We haven't done anything to anybody. Why come after us?" he asked as much to himself as to the others.

Jed Cranepool cut in. "Fact is, it's been so quiet

and peaceful, we got careless. We'd have paid hard except for you," the man said. "That calls for a specially good breakfast, I'd say."

"Sounds good to me," Fargo said, and followed the others into the center cabin.

The women fixed hot biscuits, good coffee, and pork sausages, and the families crowded together in the one cabin. Seth Hawkins said a prayerful grace of thanks and everyone pitched into their food. Fargo ate well, watched, listened as everyone spoke their mind, full of nervous relief at being alive. They were convinced the attack had come because they were there, with no more special reason than that. They'd done nothing to bring the attack on themselves, Fargo was convinced. They weren't lying to him, holding back. They weren't that kind. When he finally took his leave, he hoped they were right in their convictions. But as he slowly rode out of the little valley he knew there'd been something more. It had been no random attack. Something had triggered it, made the Crow choose the three families.

He created the slope with the nagging feeling that he'd find out why and be sorry for it.

2

Fargo headed the pinto north once again, found a cluster of box elder, and lay down to a few hours' rest as the morning sun heated the land. It was noon when he woke, refreshed; he swung onto the pinto and headed out again, this time at a fast trot. Maybe he'd get lucky and reach Prairie Dog before anything else got in the way, he told himself.

He made good time as he crossed the gently rolling land with slopes studded with oak, box elder, and red ash. He rode with his eyes sweeping back and forth over the distant ridges, along the timber stands, reading the way of a leaf, the lay of a blade of grass, the turn of a print in the soil, and a hundred more little things that made the land talk to him with a myriad of unspoken messages.

The land was calm, almost too calm, but he didn't complain any and kept his steady pace, began to let himself grow hopeful about reaching Prairie Dog. Dolly Westin's letter in his jacket pocket still gave off the faint scent of perfume under the hot sun, and Fargo chuckled to himself. Dolly had soaked the notepaper with the perfume. She always did with her notes. And he remembered how she always overused the stuff. He sniffed the faint scent. It was better than the cheap stuff she used to use, he grunted. But then Dolly had done well for herself.

She could afford the good stuff now. She was mayor of Prairie Dog.

He heard his own small chuckle. From sometime dance-hall girl to mayor. Maybe being mayor of a town such as Prairie Dog wasn't a hell of a lot, but then, how many lady mayors were there anywhere? He knew how Dolly had done it. She had spelled it out for him one night. "Find out the wrong things about the right people and you can go wherever you want," she'd said, and Dolly had followed through on that, he thought, smiling. He rode on in a good, steady pace, then he suddenly pulled the horse up sharply. He'd smelled it before he saw it, and the odor was enough to make his lips draw back at once: the sharp, unmistakable odor of charred wood. He followed his nose, edged the Ovaro around the corner of a cluster of wild cherry, and stared at the remains of the lone Conestoga, burned down to its oak axles.

He slowly dismounted, his eyes sweeping the area, returning to the bodies near the wagon: a man, two women, and two little boys about nine or ten, it was hard to tell with their necks broken as though they were chickens. Three arrows had taken care of the man. One of the two women had taken an arrow through the heart, the other had been less lucky. They'd enjoyed her first, he saw from the position of her body, then taken her scalp. Fargo's eyes scanned the ground, saw the hoofprints as they had approached the wagon. Two Indian ponies. The two Crow that had fled the cabins had found a chance to vent their fury and frustration.

Fargo walked around the wagon, found the half-burned toolbox and a shovel that had fallen to the ground. He took the shovel, dug a single grave. It seemed not just simpler, but fitting. They'd come to this land together, they'd rest together. When he finished, the sun was in the afternoon sky and he was filled with weariness and anger, weariness at having done the same thing too often and anger at the waste of lives, the stupidity of those who came out here like so many innocents, with no real understanding of the red man's rage. A savage attack on a lone wagon was common enough, but his thoughts went back to the three cabins. No random attack, he muttered again. Something dark and deadly stirred in the land, he was certain.

He mounted the Ovaro and turned the horse north, rode on with wariness and weariness, two companions he wished weren't so constant. He'd ridden into the late afternoon when he halted at a stream that meandered through a bed of chickweed; he let the Ovaro rest, drink, and cool its ankles. The horse had just lifted its head, satisfied and with thirst quenched, when Fargo spotted the spiral of dust moving toward him just over a low hillock. His eyes narrowed, stayed on the dust. The spiral moved steadily and his hands tightened on the reins, stayed poised, ready to send the horse racing away. The spiral continued to come closer and Fargo let the reins slip down from his grip. No Indians, he murmured, too much dust and the spiral rising high, heavy at the center, the kind of dust thrown up by horseshoes.

No passel of riders bunched together, either, he grunted. The spiral stayed steadily narrow. Cavalry, he said silently, riding in a column. He moved the Ovaro across the stream when the little triangular platoon pennant came into view at the top of a lance: a large, white block-letter B against a dark-blue background. Troop B crested the hillock moments after, riding in a column of twos, ten troopers and a lieutenant. As he watched, the cavalry troop slowed, turned, and headed toward him. Fargo kept riding slowly until the troop came to a halt in front of him, the lieutenant's uniform dust-streaked, his young face showing signs of saddle fatigue. His troopers echoed the same sign in faces equally young. He waited as the lieutenant surveyed him, his eyes going to the Ovaro and back again to his face.

"You're Fargo," the officer said.

"Could be. What makes you say so?" the Trails-man answered calmly.

"You fit the description the major gave me, especially that Ovaro," the lieutenant said.

"You get the cigar. Now why'd this major give you a description of me?" Fargo questioned.

"Major Keyser wants to see you. He's had us out riding the whole countryside for two days looking for you," the young officer said. "I'm Lieutenant Ryan. I'm ordered to bring you to Major Keyser."

"I'm on my way someplace," Fargo said.

The lieutenant looked uncomfortable. "I'm sorry, sir, but the major told me to bring you in. It's very important," he said.

Fargo turned thoughts in his mind. They'd no right to order him to go with them. But the army made its own rules out here in the territories. Besides, the lieutenant was only following orders, not too happily, Fargo noted. "How far? I'm not going way the hell out of my way," he said.

"Just up a ways. There's a command post at Stonemill, just this side of the Moreau," the lieutenant said.

"Let's go. We've wasted enough of my time already," Fargo growled, swung in just behind Lieutenant Ryan as the officer turned his dark bay mount and set off.

22

Dammit, Fargo swore silently. Dolly Westin was getting to be like a mirage you knew was there but couldn't reach. He rode in silence behind the lieutenant and the command post at Stonemill finally came into sight, a small stockade built around a few log buildings. He noted perhaps another fifteen troopers inside the stockade as they entered. He swung from the Ovaro as the lieutenant halted outside one of the log houses, hurried inside, and returned to beckon. Fargo sauntered into the house, his instant glance taking in a room that was half-office, half-living quarters with a worn settee and an old desk. The man behind the desk was tall, trim, his uniform well-fitted, an army career man, Fargo commented to himself.

"I'm Major Keyser," the man said. "Please sit down. I'm sorry I had to bring you in like this. Missed you at Dustyville by a few hours."

"I told the lieutenant, I'm on my way somewhere," Fargo said.

"It may have to wait," Major Keyser said. He had a face as trim as his uniform, Fargo decided, close-cropped steel-gray hair, small features evenly placed, a tight, orderly face. "There's a hell of a lot of trouble brewing. I'm told you might be the man who could stop it," the major said. "There's a campaign to send the whole, damn Indian population on the warpath."

Fargo eyed the man. "A campaign?" he echoed.

"Nothing else to call it," Major Keyser said. "There have been a series of systematic attacks on the Sioux, the Crow, and the Arapaho, hit-and-run attacks on small camps and on small hunting parties, all aimed at stirring up trouble."

"How do you come to know all this?" Fargo questioned.

"We've some half-breed informants and trading-post Indians who talk. They've told about the attacks," the major said. "And we've seen the results in the sudden increase in Indian attacks on settlers. We know of nine such recent attacks."

"Ten," Fargo said harshly as his thoughts leaped to the three cabins. He'd been right all along. No random target but specific retaliation.

The major's brows lifted but he didn't pursue the remark. "So far the Indians have replied with a tooth-for-a-tooth retaliation," he said. "But we've learned that a wholesale uprising is coming damn close. By God, we're not equipped to handle that. All hell will explode if they all take to the warpath. There'll be slaughter and massacre from one end of the territory to the other. There's no way we here at Troop B could contain it."

Fargo's lips pursed. "Somebody's got to be back of it. There's got to be a why and a what-for?"

"We've nothing you could call a lead, but there is one man, Sam Rawley," Major Keyser said.

"Why him?" Fargo asked.

"He wants to lay claim to all the land he can, but the government hasn't released any yet for claims and the Government Landholders Act says anyone living on land has first call to claim it and up to a hundred acres adjoining," the major said.

Fargo's thoughts leapfrogged over the major's words. "If the Indians slaughter damn near all the settlers, there'll be no one there to claim the land when the time comes," he muttered.

"Exactly. And nobody could accuse Sam Rawley of killing off people. The damn Indians did it all," Major Keyser said.

"Any proof besides all this thinking?" Fargo asked.

"No, except that Sam Rawley runs a small spread

and he's about the only one around here with the hands to mount these raids," Major Keyser answered. He pulled a map from beneath a blotter atop the desk, pointed to a series of checks made on it. "The raids on the Indian camps have more or less taken place following the line of these checks. Sam Rawley's spread is down from the center of this half-circle, in the perfect spot to send out raiders and get them back."

Fargo's thoughts lingered on the major's surmising for a moment. It was possible, and yet it didn't fit right, not yet anyway, too many big holes that needed answering. But he said nothing more. The major was satisfied with his theory. Maybe because it was all he had. "Why'd you haul me up here?" he asked.

"To stop these attacks on the Indian camps before it's too late," Major Keyser said with a tinge of righteousness in his tone. "Stop them, trail the men involved, get me the proof I need," he added.

"How am I going to do that when you can't?" Fargo frowned.

"Our patrols are too visible, too easily avoided. We've tried and come up empty-handed. But one man, you, could follow, trail them, find out who they are, and most important, stop any more attacks on the tribes," Major Keyser said.

Fargo grunted derisively. "That's a damn lot of supposing," he said. "Still doesn't say why you came looking for me."

Major Keyser picked a piece of paper from his desk, stared down at it. "I'm informed you're the very best there is. You're called the Trailsman," the major said. "You're the man we need."

"Forget it," Fargo said.

The major's eyes stared back in disapproval.

"There's a wholesale massacre in the making. Doesn't that mean anything to you?" he exploded, the righteousness hard in his voice again.

"Means I ought to get my ass out of here," Fargo said.

"Haven't you any sense of responsibility? You ought to have the decency to volunteer with what's at stake here," the major said.

"I've got the decency. I haven't got the idiocy," Fargo said.

"Don't you have any feelings for the innocent people who will be slaughtered?" the major demanded.

Fargo's eyes hardened at once. "I don't want to see anybody slaughtered, but let's keep the record straight. Most of these people aren't innocent. Some may be good people, some less, but they aren't innocent. They came out here to buck the odds, to take the red man's land and hold it. They figured their chances and made their choices. The only innocent ones are the kids. They didn't ask to come. They didn't ask to have their lives put on the line. So let's keep it straight."

"Keeping it straight doesn't change the facts that there'll be wholesale slaughter," Major Keyser shot back. His eyes went down to the paper in his hand. "You've scouted for the army before," he said.

"Scouted and other things." Fargo nodded. "For hard cash."

Major Keyser's trim face took on icy disapproval. "Of course, for hard cash," he almost sneered. "I'm authorized to pay for any special scouts or other civilian help I deem necessary. I'm offering five hundred dollars, Fargo, United States currency. That's a lot of money."

Fargo's lips pursed. "It is," he agreed. "It's a lot of job you're asking, too."

Righteous disapproval stayed in Major Keyser's face as he stared at the big man with the lake-blue eyes. "I must have an answer now, Mr. Fargo," he said.

"Where's the money?" Fargo said, letting a long sigh escape him. "That's too much to walk away from."

The major bent down, opened a locked drawer of his desk, drew out an iron strongbox, pulled the top up, and took out the money. He counted it, his face tight-lipped, and handed it to the big man.

Fargo took it, pushed it into his trouser pocket.

"Aren't you going to count it?" Major Keyser asked, surprised.

"No need. I don't figure you're the kind to cheat hired help." Fargo smiled.

The disapproval stayed in the major's long, hard stare. "I'm afraid I don't understand your kind of man," he intoned.

"What kind is that?" Fargo asked.

"The kind of man who lets cash and not conscience guide him," the major snapped. He didn't pick up the hard edge to the big man's smile.

"Meaning no disrespect, sir, but you're an asshole," Fargo said, and saw the major's jaw drop open. "You think this five hundred bucks is worth my neck? This money is so I can look in the mirror and tell myself that I'm not a complete damn fool. This money is so I can say to myself, 'Fargo, you're getting more than a lot of nice words and maybe a good tombstone out of this.' "

"Then why'd you agree to do it?" the officer asked.

"For the kids and for those few who came with

27

too many dreams and not enough common sense," Fargo snapped as he started from the room.

"How will you start?" Major Keyser called after him. "Follow the line I showed you on the map and pick up tracks?"

Fargo looked pained. "That's the hard way. I've other ideas," he said.

The major's eyes questioned.

"You want a fox? You find a henhouse and wait by it," Fargo snapped, and strode from the room.

Outside, he secured the money in a small pouch hidden under the cantle of his saddle and swung onto the Ovaro. He'd just wheeled the horse around when Major Keyser appeared in the doorway. "I feel I must remind you, Fargo, that you are working for the United States army now and subject to army discipline," the major said.

"Hell, I am," Fargo said almost affably. "You hired me to do a job, no more, no less. File that discipline stuff under horseshit." He spurred the pinto forward, rode from the stockade, and let his mind shuffle through the few things the major had told him. Sam Rawley would stay a big question mark for the time being, even though he was the logical choice in the major's eyes. But the map he'd been shown had revealed more than a half-circle of attacks to his quick eyes. It showed that the raiders had hit at small camps, none of the raids against large, well-protected home camps. More important, they were on camps that gave the attackers plenty of room to hit and run.

The attacks were plainly accomplishing their aim. The retaliation on the three cabins had showed that and he knew the Indian well enough to realize that there was a short fuse burning in the Dakota Territory. He turned the Ovaro north by east, thought of Dolly Westin for a moment. Visiting Dolly was not entirely out of the question yet, he told himself as he rode steadily and scanned the ground until he picked up enough fresh prints of unshod Indian ponies to follow. The prints moved back and forth over the flat land. The riders had been hunting, searching, but they slowly edged their way toward an area where the land rose in terraced ridges well covered with elm and chokecherry with serviceberry on the top ridges.

The prints led up onto the terraced ridges and Fargo moved through the elms, no longer concerned with the prints. He'd smelled the camp already, up on the second terraced ridge, the heavy odor of buffalo and elk skins being dried, the scent of smoke and fish oil.

He dismounted, moved silently through the elms, and climbed up onto the next terrace of land while letting his nose keep him on course. He was on the higher terrace when he came into sight of the camp below, larger than he'd expected with four tepees. Sioux, he saw at once, a hunting camp, no naked kids, no families, only braves and a handful of old-crone squaws brought along to tend to the hides. As he watched from a crouch, he saw a tall Sioux emerge from one of the tepees, a single eagle feather in his hair, a white choker around his neck embroidered with white and red beads.

The others gave him instant deference as he walked to where two buffalo hides were strung on a wooden drying rack, examined the skins, nodded in approval. One of the squaws brought him a bowl of gruel and he ate with his fingers and somehow managed to seem proper and neat. Chief, Fargo grunted. Young but a chief.

Fargo backed the pinto through the trees, headed

up the next two terraced ridges. The top one grew less wooded, rocks rising in ordered rows. He found a place that let him see out across the distant hills and the flat land. He let the Ovaro stand tied to the ground with reins hanging loose and sat down against one of the rocks at the end of a line of similar stones. Slowly, methodically, his gaze moved from one side of the horizon to the other and back, relentlessly, eyes straining across the hills and flat land, the timbered stands and rock outcrops, watching the sway of trees, the motion of brush, the shadows and lights that played across the land. The afternoon had grown long and he hadn't relaxed his concentration for an instant when he felt himself suddenly tense, the hairs on the back of his hands growing stiff. Movement, near the top of a low hill, becoming figures on horseback, two riders, halting at the top of the hill.

Fargo leaned forward, his gaze on the distant riders and his lips tight together as he saw two more riders approaching from the east. His gaze shifted, and he was waiting as the three horsemen appeared from west on the hill. One more arrived and the knot of riders had grown to eight. Fargo nodded, his lips pursed. Clever enough, he grunted, gathering in small units from different places. He was leaning forward as the riders started down from the top of the distant hill. They went out of sight in a line of elm that timbered half the hill, and Fargo rose to his feet. The riders would reappear where the trees ended near the bottom of the hill. They'd be moving toward the Sioux camp when they reappeared, he was certain, and he waited, eyes, ears, all his senses completely concentrated on the distant hillside.

When he heard the faint sound behind him, he

knew he was too late, but he tried for his gun, halted as the knife pressed into the back of his neck, cold, sharp, a steady, unwavering pressure. He cursed silently at himself. He'd been too absorbed in watching the distant riders—a mistake, and one paid for mistakes. The Sioux, silent as any wild hunter, had easily crept up on him. He felt a hand take the Colt from its holster and another Indian appeared in front of him, arrow drawn on bowstring and aimed at his gut. The Sioux holding the knife against his neck didn't waver the pressure and Fargo was grateful that he knew the Sioux tongue. He wondered if the two Sioux had just come upon him by chance or if they'd seen him from below. Not that it mattered much now. He was theirs and that was what mattered.

"Walk," the Sioux with the arrow aimed at him ordered.

Fargo obeyed and the Indians took him down a narrow rocky crevice, the one keeping the knife against the back of his neck. He never lessened the pressure until Fargo was at the bottom of the hill, walking into the Sioux camp. He stepped back then and Fargo half-turned to see a short, powerfully built figure. Other Indians rose, came forward to gather around the captive intruder, some with only surprise and curiosity in their faces, others with instant hostility. The tall Sioux with the wide, beaded choker came out of one of the tepees.

The one who'd held the knife gestured to the top of the terraced ridges. "He was up there, watching," he said to the tall Sioux.

The Sioux chief's black eyes focused on the big white man. He started to use sign language.

"I speak the Sioux tongue," Fargo said, and saw the Indian's eyes flicker with surprise.

31

"Why do you watch?" the Indian asked.

Fargo's smile was wry. "You will not believe this," he muttered, and saw the Sioux's frown of incomprehension. He used the Sioux he knew and added sign language to make his point. "I was waiting to protect you," he said.

"He lies," one of the others shouted.

Fargo shook his head. "No lie," he said. His glance moved to the right as he saw another Sioux appear leading the Ovaro. The tall Indian's eyes looked at the horse with instant approval. "What are you called?" Fargo asked.

"Two Beavers," the Indian answered. "I am chief of the Red Valley Sioux." The chief's eyes narrowed as he peered at Fargo. "You are one of those who raid our camps," he said.

"No, but they come soon," Fargo said. "I watched. I came to warn you."

"You lie with a quick tongue," the Sioux said.

"They'll come. You'll see I speak the truth," Fargo said.

"He lies," someone shouted again.

"What if he is right? What if he is one of them?" Two Beavers said to the others. "Double the sentries. Bring the horses near. We will wait and be ready."

"I'm not one of them. I came to stop the attacks," Fargo insisted, even as he swore silently at the Indian's disbelief.

"Tie him," Two Beavers ordered.

Fargo felt his arms pulled back behind him at once, leather thongs wrapped around his wrists and ankles. Considerably less than gently, they threw him to the ground, pushed him up against a tree. He saw the Sioux that had taken his gun brandishing the Colt as though it were a newfound toy.

Fargo wriggled himself onto his side so he could

watch and he saw the Sioux horsemen ride out in the last light of the day. Others brought their ponies near and crouched down to wait, bows in hand. The Ovaro, he saw, was tethered with the extra ponies to one side. He swore again, softly, as the day closed down and there was still no attack. He had to wonder if he'd been wrong about the distant horsemen and angrily flung aside the thought. He hadn't been wrong, he told himself, not with the way they had gathered, within easy range of the Indian camp. It was too planned, and it was with a grim kind of satisfaction that he heard the sudden sharp sound of gunfire. The camp sprang into life as it became clear that the extra sentries had intercepted the attackers. He watched the other Sioux sweep from the camp on their horses to disappear into the darkness and the trees.

Two Beavers stood beside the tepee, flanked by three of his warriors, and Fargo listened to the distant gunfire. It was growing erratic, too rapid, the attackers firing as they ran.

"Let me go, dammit," he called to the Indian chief. "I want to go after them. I can find out where they're going." The Indian's glance at him was one of pure scorn. "Goddamn, let me go after them," Fargo shouted again even as he knew it was but a waste of breath.

The chief's gaze returned to the darkness and waiting, and Fargo heard the rifle fire die away. His eyes were on the trees as he heard the sound of the horses racing back, watched the Indians sweep into the camp with triumphant shouts, bows raised in the air.

"They run . . . all run," one brave shouted at Two Beavers as he leaped from his horse. "They wanted to take us by surprise." The Indian laughed as he made the sign for turning things around.

Fargo used his feet to shift his body against the tree and he felt the frustration searing him inside. "Let me go after them. I came to help you," he called. "You have proof now."

The chief frowned at him. "Proof?" he echoed.

"I said they'd attack. I said they were coming," Fargo answered.

"You knew because you were sent ahead to scout our camp and signal them to come in," Two Beavers returned.

"No, I was there to stop the attack," Fargo insisted.

"I would be laughed from the tribes for believing such a story from a white-eyes," the Sioux said.

"It's the truth," Fargo said.

"The white-eyes have been raiding. They want trouble," the Indian said. "They will have it."

"No, not all white men. Only some," Fargo tried again. "Others want to stop the attacks on the tribes."

The Indian chief's frown grew deeper. "The white-eyes care about the safety of the Sioux?" he asked, and the question was cloaked in derision.

Rightfully so, Fargo grunted inwardly. The army didn't give a damn about the Indians. It was strictly enlightened self-interest, the attempt to head off what they knew they couldn't handle. Simple enough, yet not to the Sioux, a concept impossible to explain in any way the Indian would understand and believe. Fargo swore inwardly and lapsed into angry silence.

"You die at dawn. Slowly," the Sioux chieftain said. "See to his bonds," he ordered the others as he went into his tepee. Two Indians went to Fargo, one the short figure that still had the Colt tucked into the band of his loincloth.

Fargo felt himself rolled over, his wrist and ankle bonds inspected, tested to their satisfaction. The short Sioux kicked him in the side and sent him rolling against a tree, and Fargo drew breath in sharply at the stab of pain in his ribs. He lay still against the tree and watched the two Indians walk away. His eyes scanned the camp as the horses were tethered to one side, the Ovaro in front, and he watched the encampment settle down for the night. The handful of squaws went into one tepee and most of the braves disappeared into the others, but a half-dozen lay down in the open ground. One was the short Sioux with his Colt and he watched the Indian settle himself a half-dozen yards from him.

Fargo stayed motionless, watched the moon slowly rise over the trees. Dawn would come too damn soon, he knew, but he made himself lie still until the camp was deep in sleep.

Finally, his eyes scanning the sleeping figures one more time, he drew his legs up all the way until he was almost in the position of an unborn baby. He could just reach his legs with his fingers and he felt the strain on leg muscles pulled tight. He pushed his right trouser leg up—a slow, painfully slow effort—felt the smoothness of the narrow holster strapped to his calf. Inside, the thin, narrow, twin-bladed throwing knife rested, and working his fingers with painstaking care, he got a precarious grip on the handle of the knife. He pulled slowly, felt the knife sliding from the holster, halted, got a better grip on the handle with the tips of his fingers. The knife came out all the way and he gripped the handle with his right hand, twisting his wrists inside the leather thongs.

He pushed his legs straight as they began to cramp on him, stayed still, and let the muscles stretch back into place. Carefully he turned the knife in his hand, positioned the blade edge against the leather thongs, and began to slide the blade back and forth on the thongs. A sawing motion, but he spat derisively at the word. His bound wrists allowed for very little sawing and almost no pressure on the straps. His bonds let him move the blade only a fraction of an inch at a time. It would have to do, he told himself as he settled down to the slow, careful process. He found he had to halt every few minutes as his forearm muscles cramped at the unnatural strain.

He had made only a tiny cut in the leather thongs as he watched the moon rise higher, move slowly across the sky, slowly but inexorably, and he had to pause again, let his forearm muscles uncramp. Would he be able to cut through the thongs by dawn? he had to ask himself as he continued with the agonizingly slow task. Back and forth, tiny, inching motions of the twin-edged blade, and the leather thongs still bore only a small cut.

Fargo lay on his side, stayed grimly at the task, and cursed as he saw the moon dropping behind the low hills in the distance. He transferred the knife into his left hand, used the tips of his fingers to feel the cut he had made. Halfway, he guessed, but the leather was cut, starting to give way and he could feel the tiny shreds on his fingertips. He began to saw again with the inching strokes, cursed at each halt he had to make as his arm muscles grew more and more strained.

He halted, flexed his arm and wrist muscles, and

felt the thongs move, give a fraction. He did it again and the leather stretched a fraction more. But he was working with fractions, inches, and he'd stretched the thongs enough to give him a little more room to work. He could bring a little pressure to bear on the blade edge as he sawed it back and forth again. When he paused next, little beads of perspiration coating his forehead, he saw the moon had gone from sight, the sky in that hanging blackness just before dawn. But the cut in the thongs was deeper. He worked a few minutes more, pulled the blade back, and once more stretched his arms, strained deltoids, biceps, forearm radials; and he felt the thongs stretch, break with a suddenness that made his arms fly apart. He brought them back together behind him at once, his gaze on the sleeping figures. No one had stirred, sleep still heavy on them.

Slowly he brought his arms around in front of him, let them rest there, restore themselves, the crampled muscles throbbing. After a few minutes, he reached down to the thongs binding his ankles, cut with the double-edged blade, now able to use pressure and movement. It still took another five minutes before the sinewy leather gave way and he saw the sky starting to turn gray as dawn slid its way over the horizon. He stretched his ankles, let circulation flow back into them, waited until he was sure they'd hold up, and drew himself to a crouch. The short Sioux was nearest, the Colt beside the man on the ground.

Fargo rose, took a half-dozen long steps, and was beside the sleeping Sioux. He reached down, had the Colt in his hand when the Indian's senses stabbed at him. Fargo saw the man's eyes come open, his head start to lift. The barrel of the heavy

Colt came down in a short blow but with all Fargo's strength in it. The Indian's head fell backward as a river of red suddenly coursed down from the top of his hairline, his eyes closing at once. Fargo stayed in the half-crouch, his lips a thin line. The others were stirring as the sky grew lighter. He ran on silent footsteps in a long, loping crouch, reached the Ovaro, and swung into the saddle, pulling the horse's reins free of a branch in one motion.

He saw two of the figures outside the tepee sit, still half-asleep, and at the same moment the tall figure of the Sioux chieftain stepped from the tepee. Two Beavers started to sweep the camp with a glance and Fargo dug heels into the Ovaro. The horse charged at a full gallop, straight at the tepee. Fargo saw the Sioux leader start to turn to dart into the tent, but the horse was at him, pulling up sharply at Fargo's command. Fargo, leaning sideways in the saddle, reached one hand down, seized the Indian by the man's long, black hair, almost lost his grip on the bear-oiled slickness of it, but twisted, held on.

Two Beavers gave a short cry of pain as Fargo almost yanked him from his feet by his hair and the Indian felt the muzzle of the Colt against his cheekbone. Fargo saw the others, awake now, standing, move toward him, halt as still more ran from their tepees.

"Come after me and you'll need a new chief," Fargo said, though words were not necessary as the Sioux stayed back, faces glowering with anger in the new day, yet not daring to rush him. "Stay back," Fargo warned again. "Don't follow or I blow his head away."

They understood all too well and Fargo moved the Ovaro slowly, backing the horse, pulling the

Indian chieftain with him by the hair. Once in tree cover, he turned the Ovaro, moved the horse into a trot, not releasing his grip on the Sioux. Two Beavers turned his body to run alongside the horse as Fargo rode, holding his grip on the Indian's hair and keeping the Colt against his temple now. The Indian could easily keep up with the horse's slow trot for a little while, he knew, and he pushed his way down the terraced ridge as the dawn grew stronger. He felt the Indian try to twist away, tightened his grip on the man's hair. "Once more and I shoot," he warned.

The Sioux chieftain trotting beside the horse cast a glance of arrogance and hate at his captor. "You will not shoot me yet," he said.

"Why the hell not?" Fargo barked.

"They will come when they hear the shot. They will have no reason to stay back then. You want more distance from them before you shoot," the Sioux said.

Fargo swore and knew he oughtn't to have been surprised. The Sioux had the craft of hunter and hunted, the primal knowledge of how all creatures behaved. "Just keep running," he snapped as he increased the pinto's speed.

He reached the lowest of the terraced ridges when he reined up sharply, flung the Indian from him as he did. He saw the Indian hit the ground, spin, stare up at him, wait for the shot that would kill him, his face impassive. Fargo's finger held on the trigger of the Colt. He was supposed to keep the peace, not inflame things more. Sparing the Sioux chieftain might be a meaningless act, the reservoir of hate too deep for a single, grand gesture. But then it might help a little to keep back the wave of rage that was close to painting the Dakota Territory red. Killing the chieftain would certainly help speed up the eventual explosion.

He lowered the gun, turned the Ovaro, and started to ride on. He cast a glance back at the Sioux. The Indian was standing, looking after him, his face wreathed in perplexed uncertainty. Fargo spurred the pinto on. Mercy was not a word in the Indian vocabulary. Honor, discipline, revenge, justice, even forgiveness, but only when earned, those words the Indian understood. But not mercy. Fargo left the Indian frowning after him as he raced the pinto down the slope and across the flat land as the sun came up.

He rode a few miles with his eyes on the ground, trying to pick up the prints of those who had fled, but finally gave it up as an impossible task. Besides, they'd undoubtedly separated anyway. He found a pair of good, wide box elders, perfect shade trees, and lay down under the coolness of their leafy canopy. He slept hard and let rest restore the strain of the night on body and spirit.

3

It was past noon when he woke, found a small freshwater pond, and decided to wash the trail dust from himself. He lay the big Sharps at the edge of the pond as he stripped, bathed, enjoyed the cool of the water. It was a good place to enjoy a bath, the land flat in all directions, no chance for anyone to sneak up, and he luxuriated in the water, then climbed out to sit naked on the grass and let the sun dry off his glistening muscles and lean, hard body.

The last twenty-four hours hadn't gone right, none of it, the only saving grace was that the raid on the Sioux had been turned aside. His eyes narrowed in thought as he stretched, leaned back on the grass. Whoever was back of the raids had a better-than-average knowledge of where the Indians set up their small camps. Someone who knew the land and knew the Indian, and that could eliminate a lot of people who knew the first but not really the second. The Indian moved small hunting and fishing camps, yet he returned to the same general area. Habits were ingrained in the red man as well as the white. A good site for a hunting camp, or a good place to tan and store hides, was a place to return to when the time came around.

That still meant someone damned familiar with

the Indian ways, and Fargo's thoughts drifted to Sam Rawley. The major was certain Sam Rawley knew those things, that he was a man with knowledge as well as motive, and Fargo felt the small stab of irritation push at him. Perhaps the major was right, but something still didn't fit right. He'd be taking a closer look at Sam Rawley for himself, he was certain. But not yet. Right now, Rawley knew only that Major Keyser and his troops searched for the raiders. He'd like to leave it that way, Fargo pondered. A visit could put the man on guard. If he had anything to be on guard about, Fargo added quickly.

He pushed himself up on his elbows, felt warm and dried thoroughly, and he rose, dressed, and climbed onto the pinto. He set out across the flat land, rode north, and felt the temptation to keep on as he thought of Prairie Dog with Dolly Westin waiting there. But he turned west, followed the curve of a line of distant elm and box elder. The map Major Keyser had shown him was etched in his mind, and the distant trees were an extension of the half-circle where the Indian camps had been raided and marked on the map. Fargo noted enough unshod hoofprints to tell him that the trees sheltered other Indian encampments.

He swung the horse a little closer to the trees, then veered off again to ride up a long, low hill. He paused, spotted a thin line of smoke, saw two cabins in the distance, squinted, and made out two men working the land near with hand plows. He rode on and his mouth turned hard as he thought of a full Indian uprising. Settlers such as these wouldn't stand a chance. He found himself thinking about the motives Major Keyser had given Sam Rawley. He couldn't dismiss them. Greed for land was a powerful, driving force. But to bring on a wholesale massacre smelled of something more than simple greed. Yet he couldn't dismiss the motive. He'd seen what greed could do to men.

He broke off speculation as he spotted the column of dust on the horizon line of a low hill. The dust rose straight into a windless sky, moved steadily just below the top of the hill. Fargo frowned. The dust had a familiar shape and movement to it, the steady, thin movement of a cavalry platoon in a column of twos. His frown deepened. Major Keyser's troopers? They were far west of where the major had his patrol lines.

Fargo moved the Ovaro forward, up the long, low hill to the top, and halted to gaze down the other side of the gentle slope at the cavalry troop riding in a column of twos with an officer at the head.

He saw the troop swing, start toward him with increased speed, breaking into a fast canter. He waited, his eyes holding on the line of blue-clad troopers as they drew closer. Not young Lieutenant Ryan this time, he saw; it was a different officer but not much older. As the column closed on him, the dark-blue pennant carried by the lead trooper fluttered to one side and Fargo saw the white block letter against the dark blue. He felt the frown dig deeper. The letter was a D.

He was still frowning as the platoon came to a halt, the lieutenant's glance a quick appraisal, lingering on the magnificent Ovaro with its black front and hind quarters, its stark white midsection. "Lieutenant Edgars, here," the officer said. "Are you Fargo?"

"Same question gets the same answer," Fargo commented. "Could be. What makes you say so?"

43

"You fit the description, especially that Ovaro," the lieutenant said.

"I think there's an echo on this prairie," Fargo remarked.

"Beg your pardon?" Lieutenant Edgars frowned in puzzlement.

"Private joke," Fargo said. "Who sent you looking for me?"

"Colonel Davidson. He wants to see you right away," the officer said.

"Jesus, I'm the belle of the ball," Fargo growled, and the lieutenant looked puzzled again. "Where's the colonel?" Fargo asked.

"At a field camp just up past Rockfall. I'm to bring you to him at once," Edgars said.

Fargo kept his expression impassive while curiosity ran wild inside him. "Let's not keep the colonel waiting," he said. He swung in beside the lieutenant as the man turned the column of troopers around, started back the way he'd come.

"Been looking for me long?" Fargo asked casually.

"Three days now," the officer said.

"How'd the colonel know I'd be around here?" Fargo asked, choosing questions carefully.

"One of our troopers was in Dustyville for extra supplies when you brought those wagons in. He happened to mention it to the colonel and he sent us out searching the whole countryside at once," the lieutenant said.

Fargo nodded and the curiosity inside him was whirling now. But he rode on with only small talk until two tall, sharply jagged pinnacles of volcanic-like rock rose up ahead of them and he saw the field camp between them, a line of tethered army mounts, another dozen troopers, and a pup tent with the troop flag over the closed flap.

The lieutenant rode past two rifle-carrying sentries, waved his troopers on as he reined up outside the tent.

Fargo had just dismounted when the man stepped from the tent, his blue uniform collar open at the neck, his colonel's insignia marking him at once. Fargo took in a man of medium height, a graying mustache not quite covering a tight, severe mouth. Colonel Davidson had intense blue eyes that made him seem to stare fiercely, and his tight-skinned face held more than a hint of arrogance. It was the face of a man used to being obeyed and having his own way.

"Fargo, sir," Lieutenant Edgars said, stepped back, and hurried away.

"About time," Colonel Davidson snapped, his gaze boring in on the big man in front of him. "I'm Colonel Davidson, Fargo. Got a little job for you."

"Why me?" Fargo asked.

Colonel Davidson smiled and it was a cold, almost crafty caricature of a smile. "Because you're the man for it. I know all about you, Fargo. I was line officer when General Peterson called you in for that special job at Sunwater. I'm sure you remember that."

"I remember," Fargo said laconically.

"The general told me that you're a hard man to handle, but the very best there is," Colonel Davidson said. "That's why when I heard you were in Dustyville, I had my troopers out looking for you."

"Why?" Fargo asked.

"I told you, I've a special job for you," Colonel Davidson said. "The tribes are ready to take the warpath."

"I heard," Fargo said.

"Somebody's been stirring them up," the colonel said.

"Heard that too," Fargo answered.

"Then you know the army doesn't have the men to handle it," Colonel Davidson said crisply. "I've been ordered by Washington to set up a patrol line running southwest to try to protect those settlements below it. I'm on my way to do that right now. Everybody's been given special orders in a hurry." Fargo nodded, waited as the colonel paused. "But my daughter's been out visiting me. She's with me now. I'm not taking her with me to set up a patrol line. I want her out of here, safe, far enough away, at Fort Kearny in Wyoming. I can't spare a man to take her, and it'd be against army rules without official permission."

"You could put her up with one of the families settled back of your patrol line," Fargo suggested.

"No, dammit," Colonel Davidson exploded. "And have her massacred with them? There's every chance of that and you know it."

Fargo didn't disagree and the colonel's face grew hard as he bit out words. "I want my daughter safe, understand? My little girl's not going to be massacred. You'll take her to Fort Kearny in Wyoming, get her safe away from here, and you'll get top dollar for the job."

"I've got a job," Fargo said, and saw the surprise come into the man's eyes. "Major Keyser hired me to find out who's stirring up the tribes and try to stop them before it's too late."

Colonel Davidson's frowning stare held on the big man. "Keyser's stupid. It's too late now anyway," he snapped.

"The major thinks otherwise." Fargo shrugged.

"What'd he offer you?" Colonel Davidson questioned.

"Five hundred U.S. dollars," Fargo answered.

"I'll give you six hundred right here and now. Forget about Major Keyser's orders. I'm giving you new ones," the colonel said.

"He's paid me," Fargo said.

"You can send him his money back by post later," the colonel said.

Fargo's stare at the colonel was penetrating. "What if I could find out who's back of it and stop it?" he asked.

"Forget it. It'd take too long. Let him hire somebody else," the man said.

"You know he can't do that now," Fargo answered.

"I don't care. But my daughter, my little girl, is going to be safe, that's what I care about and I want you to see her safe at Fort Kearny," the man said.

Fargo probed into the man with his remarks. "Major Keyser will be thinking I'm out trying to do what he ordered me to do," Fargo said.

"I told you to forget about Major Keyser," the colonel snapped. "I outrank him and I'm countermanding his orders. Six hundred dollars' worth of countermanding. That's a damn lot of money, Fargo."

"It is," Fargo agreed.

"But it's worth it to have my little girl safe," the colonel said.

Fargo let his lips purse. He'd probed into the man and he didn't like the answers he'd gotten. He'd not be sending money back to Major Keyser by post. Sending money back was against his principles. Besides, he'd already earned some of it last night. He smiled inwardly, as his thoughts leapfrogged. Six hundred was more than five hundred, and together they made over a thousand. Now that was a right respectable sum, he decided. His eyes stayed on Colonel Davidson as he concluded that he'd quickly come to dislike the man. But turning away good cash was as much against his principles as sending it back. The colonel could use a lesson and he could use eleven hundred dollars much more than five. Fargo continued to smile to himself.

He half-shrugged. "Why not?" he grunted. "You're the colonel."

"Now you're showing some common sense, Fargo," Colonel Davidson said. "Come inside the tent. I'll give you the money and you can meet my daughter. Her name is Janice."

The colonel pulled the tent flap open and Fargo followed him inside, halted, knew he failed to keep the surprise from his face as the girl rose from where she'd been sitting atop a keg. He saw hair the color of new wheat, a pale, ash blond; hazel eyes in a face that was more than pretty; blond eyebrows and a short, straight nose; full, very red lips that seemed almost out of place in the pastel coloring of her face. He guessed the colonel's "little girl" to be anywhere from eighteen to twenty-two. She wore a dark-green blouse that made the rest of her coloring seem even more delicate, and he noted that the fabric stretched tight over full, close-together breasts. A narrow waist flowed into modest hips wrapped in a black riding skirt. Her hazel eyes held more than a touch of her father's arrogance, Fargo noted as he saw her take him in. Maybe she wasn't used to being obeyed, but she was used to having her own way, he wagered.

"This is my little girl, Janice," the colonel said, and beamed at his daughter. Janice Davidson ignored her father as she moved her eyes over the big man with the lake-blue eyes, the intense, chiseled face, the light leanness of his powerful body. She felt the charged, sensual aura that emanated from him, saw the appreciation in his eyes. "Skye Fargo," the colonel cut in again. "The man I told you I was trying to find. He'll be taking you to Fort Kearny."

Janice Davidson allowed a tiny smile to touch the corners of her very red, full mouth. "Good," was all she said. The tiny smile, a kind of tolerant amusement, stayed as Fargo's glance paused again at her breasts, which seemed almost one line as their fullness held them against each other. Colonel Davidson had opened an army duffel bag and Fargo saw him draw out a roll of bills, hand it to him.

"It's all there. Six hundred dollars," the man said. Fargo pushed the money into a pocket. "You start now. Every minute counts," the colonel ordered.

"Two extra canteens for her," Fargo said. "And an army uniform, coat, hat, and pants, small size."

"You've a reason, I'm sure," the colonel said. "I won't waste time going into it. I'll get it. We always have some extra gear."

Fargo walked from the tent, waited beside the Ovaro. He had put the colonel's money with the major's when Janice came from behind the tent leading a standard army mount, a sturdy dark-bay Morgan. The colonel appeared soon after with the canteen, handed Fargo the uniform tied in a flat bundle. The girl kissed her father, stayed in his embrace for a long moment as he stroked the ash-blond hair; then he stepped back, turned his eyes on the big man astride the Ovaro.

"You get my little girl to Fort Kearny, Fargo, that's all I care about," the Colonel said.

"I know," Fargo grunted, wondered if Janice saw the hardness come into his eyes. "Ready?" he asked her, and she nodded, climbed onto the Morgan, and he enjoyed the way her breasts tightened the blouse as she sat straight in the saddle. He turned the Ovaro, set the horse into a trot, and rode on, not looking back, not until he was halfway up a low hillside. He saw the troopers had already struck the pup tent and he moved down onto the flat land. He was heading toward a cluster of chokecherry when Janice Davidson pulled her mount up alongside him. He speared her with a long glance.

"You're a surprise, you know," he commented. Her blond eyebrows lifted. "I expected you to be ten or twelve, the way the colonel talked about his little girl," Fargo said.

"Sorry about that." She half-chuckled. "Daddy has a way of doing that. I guess I'll always be that to him." Her hazel eyes returned a long, appraising glance. "You're a surprise, too," she said. "I expected some gray-bearded, trail-worn old codger."

"Sorry about that," Fargo echoed. "You disappointed?"

The tiny smile touched the full, red lips again. "I wouldn't say that," she answered. "Are you?"

"I'll let you know when the trip's over," he said, saw her eyes narrow a fraction. He halted under the chokecherry, his gaze distant, focused back the way they had come. It wasn't long before he saw the thin column of dust rise into the air, begin to move. The colonel had struck camp, was heading to set up his thin patrol line running southwest. Major Keyser's equally thin line would be running northeast, he mused as his lips drew back in distaste. Neither line would be enough to control a full-scale uprising, and he thought again of what that would mean. He waited till the column of dust had spiraled out of sight, Janice Davidson's voice cutting into his thoughts.

"What are you waiting for?" she asked.

"Resting my horse," he said and saw the instant skepticism in her glance. He waited another five minutes to make certain the colonel was well on his way and then he turned the Ovaro, tossed a smile at Janice Davidson. "Let's move. Got work to do," he said. He headed the Ovaro out from beneath the chokecherry and up a slope, down the other side.

Janice Davidson swung in beside him as he rode slowly, his eyes scanning the ground most of the time, peering at trailmarks, halting every once in a while to dismount and study the prints closely.

It was the third time he'd dismounted and risen from examining the prints with a frown that Janice Davidson's voice held a note of asperity. "What's the matter?" she questioned. "Shouldn't we be making more time?"

Fargo's frown stayed as he pulled himself onto the Ovaro. "Too many," he muttered.

"Too many what?" she prodded.

"Too many Indian pony tracks, too many others. Can't sort anything out," he said, his gaze still fixed on the ground.

"Why are you trying?" She frowned.

"Want to find a pattern," Fargo answered.

"Why? You're taking me to Fort Kearny," Janice Davidson said, her tone taking on a thin frosting.

"Along the way," Fargo said casually as he scanned the ground.

"Along the way?" Janice Davidson echoed, the frost in her tone growing thicker. "Exactly what does that mean?"

Fargo continued to scan the marks on the ground, but he smiled, a modest, almost-shy smile. "It means I'm sort of combining jobs," he said.

Her silence was loud and he felt her eyes boring

into him. He looked up to see her staring at him with a mixture of disbelief and astonishment. "You can't do that," Janice Davidson breathed. "You can't do that."

"Guess again," Fargo snapped, the smile vanishing from his face.

4

The hazel eyes had become burning copper. "You bastard," she hissed.

"Please, no flattery," Fargo said.

"You take me to Fort Kearny right now," Janice Davidson flung at him.

"No, not right now. When I'm finished doing what Major Keyser paid me to do, try and stop a massacre," Fargo said.

"My daddy paid you to take me to Fort Kearny," she snapped.

"So he did. I told you, I'm combining jobs," Fargo said.

"You've no scruples at all. That wasn't the deal. You heard Daddy tell you to forget about Major Keyser's orders."

Fargo's lake-blue eyes grew frosted. "I heard him," he snapped. "Your daddy's a shit."

Janice Davidson's mouth fell open and her delicate blond coloring grew flushed, a deep-pink suffusing her face. "How dare you?"

"Easy," Fargo said. "Telling me to forget about helping the major is really telling me to forget about all those people who'll be massacred as long as you're safe."

"I'm his daughter. Of course he cares about what happens to me," Janice flung back.

"Touching, but selfish," Fargo commented. "He's supposed to put duty first. That's why he's out here in that uniform. Duty is to care about the settlers, not tell me to forget about them."

"He's not selfish," Janice returned, but Fargo heard the defensiveness in her voice. "You shouldn't have taken his money if that's how you felt. You should have just refused."

Fargo made a harsh sound. "And have him press me into service? The army can do that out here in the territories, press into service any man they think they need. He wanted me and he'd have done it, probably sent three of his troopers along to see that I didn't take off. I wasn't having any of that."

"So you just lied to him and took his money. You're despicable," Janice Davidson hissed.

"I didn't lie to him. I'll get you to Fort Kearny, I told you," Fargo said.

"Unless you get me killed first," she snapped.

"I'll try not to do that." Fargo shrugged.

The hazel eyes stayed copper. "How good of you," she said with ice on each word.

"Don't mention it," Fargo returned.

"Dammit, you've no right to do this," she bit out.

"More right than Daddy has telling me to turn my back on all those people. I'm trying to head off a wholesale slaughter. Are you so much like your daddy that that doesn't mean a damn thing to you?" he tossed at her.

He saw the uncomfortableness behind the glare of her eyes. "Of course it means something to me," she snapped.

"Then shut up and come along," Fargo said.

"You go on your own. I'll go back and catch up to Daddy," Janice Davidson said.

"He's too far gone by now," Fargo said.

"I've a good horse. I'll catch up," she insisted.

"No way," Fargo said.

"I'm not riding with anyone like you," Janice said.

"Look, honey, if there was time, I'd put you someplace till I could get back to you, but there isn't. Every damn minute counts. I'm no happier than you, but that's the way it is. Now, are you coming the easy way or the hard way?" Fargo said.

Janice Davidson's hazel eyes gave him a narrowed stare, but she wheeled her horse around and fell in beside him. He cast an eye at the darkening sky, not more than an hour from nightfall; he turned the Ovaro up a hill and found a place to camp for the night before the last of the light drifted away. He dismounted in a small grove of elm at the top of a slow rise, unsaddled the Ovaro, and watched as Janice Davidson tethered her mount on the other side of the trees.

He made a small fire as the darkness descended and the night turned cool at once. He pulled out his bedroll, stretched out on it, clasped his hands behind his head, and watched Janice sit down on the other side of the fire. Weak shadows played along the undersides of her breasts where they filled the blouse, and she curled her legs under her, rested on one arm. The tiny fire reached out to deepen the ash-blond hair, the blond eyebrows and blond eyelashes with a soft, yellow glow that washed her with its softness and made her seem beautifully unreal, a gorgeous, ghostly wraith. Only the sullenness of her lovely face reminded him that she was very real and still very angry.

"I'm a very light sleeper. Don't get any ideas," he remarked quietly.

She shot an acid glance at him across the tiny fire. "So am I. Don't you get any ideas," she snapped.

He laughed. "We're talking about different kinds of escaping," he said.

"Whatever," she grunted. "Just don't get any."

"Now, what makes you think I'd have any such ideas?" he asked.

"Hah!" she snorted. "They're part of you, built in. You'd go to bed with any woman you could. I saw the way you looked at me when we first met."

"I saw the way you looked at me," he returned.

She flushed at once. "I didn't do any such thing," she denied.

"Hell you didn't," he said calmly.

"We see what we want to see," she returned waspishly.

"Bullshit, sweetie." Fargo smiled pleasantly. "You're safe, anyway." He saw the faint glint of curiosity touch her eyes. "I've never been much for breaking in green mounts," he explained affably.

Her glare became fire. "Bastard," she hissed, pulled herself to her feet, and went to her saddlebag.

He watched her take out nightclothes and disappear into the blackness of the trees. When she returned, the fire was almost out and he saw she wore a long, deep-red cotton nightdress, her ash-blond hair silvery in the faint light. She put her bedroll against a tree at the far side of the glen and lay down.

He rose, pulled off clothes, undressed to his underpants. The fire was but glowing embers now, but he could feel her eyes on his silhouette, a hard-muscled, powerful silhouette. He lay down on his bedroll and let sleep come quickly, slept as he always did, as the cougar sleeps, gathering in rest, yet his senses ever alert just below the surface of his slumber.

But the night passed quietly, no sounds to interrupt his catlike sleep, and he woke with the new sun to see Janice still curled up asleep. He used his canteen to wash, was finished and dressed when she stirred, sat up. The deep-red nightdress had come open at the top, just enough to let him see the beautiful swell of her breasts, very creamy, almost milkweedlike in color. She focused her eyes, pulled the nightdress closed, and rose to take her own canteen and vanish into the thickness of the trees. She had the same dark-green blouse on and her ash-blond hair made her as strikingly beautiful as marsh marigold. She met his eyes, saw the admiration in them, walked on to put her things in her saddlebag.

"Saw some wild plum bushes that'll make for good breakfast eating," he said as he saddled the Ovaro. She made no comment, her face set. "You can grouse the whole damn trip. Won't bother me any," he remarked.

She turned on him as she finished tightening the cinch on her mount. "Of course not. You're getting your way. You're pleased as Punch with yourself. You've taken both Major Keyser and my father. I think that's what you're enjoying, not all this noble concern over stopping a massacre," she threw at him.

Fargo regarded her with lips pursed. "You know, with a little practice, you could become a real fourteen-karat bitch," he said as he swung onto the Ovaro and rode away. He heard her follow a few minutes later and she caught up to him when he stopped at the wild plum bushes. She ate in silence, but there was no apology in the set of her face. She

57

was one of those rare women who could be sullen and remain delicately beautiful, he decided.

Finishing the plums, he remounted and started off in a slow trot, heard her follow as he moved down a slope, his eyes scanning the land. It had thickened with stands of elm and hornbeam. Beyond, the woodland grew dense, heavy with pale-barked Plains cottonwood. Indian camps back inside, he was certain, and he knew he had to get a handle on where the raiders would strike next. But the trailmarks showed nothing he could translate, and a visit to Sam Rawley seemed increasingly necessary. But it still bothered him. Whether the man was or wasn't behind the raids, a visit would take time and perhaps give him less than it did Sam Rawley. Time, he grunted, that was the key word, and it was slipping away.

He let his eyes scan the distant horizon. A high vantage point that would let him scan the entire lay of the land would help. But there was no such place, nothing high enough to afford him the clear, unobstructed view all around that he needed. The raiders held all the cards. He had just reached the base of the long slope when the lone Conestoga wagon came into view, moving slowly northwest. He squinted, saw the two men in the wagon, one riding beside it. He caught the rush of instant excitement that coursed through Janice as she sat very straight in the saddle, her breasts lifting, pushing forward to put a strain on the blouse.

"If that wagon's going to Fort Kearny, I'm going with it," she announced, casting Fargo a disapproving glance.

"If," he said.

"I'll find out," she snapped.

He shrugged. "And just as I looked forward to

getting to know you better," Fargo said, his eyes holding on the Conestoga.

"I'm sure you did," she answered, slapped her horse on the rump, and took off for the Conestoga in a canter.

Fargo let her go, followed unhurriedly, his gaze going past her to the wagon. Janice had reached the wagon and was in earnest conversation with the driver when he slowly rode up to halt. His eyes took in the three men, his handsome, chiseled face expressionless. The one with the reins in his hand was a beanpole figure with a drawn face and darting eyes that held a furtive cast to them. Beside him, the second man had thinning hair atop a face that held meanness in every feature, the downturned mouth, the hard eyes, the tight skin. Fargo's eyes went to the man on the horse, younger than the other two but with eyes older and colder than the others. He wore a big, black stetson, two pearl-handled Whitneyville Colts, polished and shined. His eyes stayed on the big man on the Ovaro, a piercing, penetrating stare.

"They're headed for Fort Kearny," Janice announced, turning to Fargo as she managed to look both smug and prim at once.

"What do you know about that?" Fargo remarked. He seemed to consider the situation as he let his brow furrow in thought. "But I promised your daddy I'd get you there myself," he said.

"A promise you've already broken," Janice said sternly. "Now the money can be yours without your having to work for it. You'll enjoy that even more, I'm sure."

"Shit, we'll take good care of the little lady," the beanpole figure said, and Fargo saw him devour the girl with his eyes. He turned an avaricious smile at her. "Janice, you said, right?" he asked, and she nodded. "It'll be a goddamn pleasure having you along."

"Hell, yes," the balding one said. "Make the whole shit trip worthwhile."

Fargo smiled, but they were too busy eyeing Janice to see the ice in it. "Where are you gents from?" he asked.

There was a moment of silence. "Minnesota," the balding one said. "We're from Minnesota way."

Fargo looked at the man with the reins as he nodded in agreement. "What's brought you out this way?" he prodded.

"Want to settle down, do us some farming, get a little patch of land," the man said.

"Yes, sir," the young one said, laughing. "Just want to get into plowin' and tillin' and pickin' weeds."

The sharp-faced man cut in, his words aimed at Janice. "Now you just tie your horse to the other two trailing back of the wagon," he said. "Then you come up here and sit beside me."

Janice turned, started toward the rear of the Conestoga.

"Then it's all settled, I guess," Fargo said.

"It's all settled," she echoed as she tied the bay behind the other two horses.

"Mind if I ride along for a spell?" Fargo asked, and saw the refusal leap into the younger one's cold eyes, but the driver answered quickly, too quickly, Fargo noted.

"Can't see any harm in that, right, boys?" the man said. The balding one mumbled agreement, the man in the saddle remained silent.

"Much obliged." Fargo smiled.

Janice strode past him with a smug glance as he

moved the Ovaro behind the Conestoga and watched her climb onto the driver's seat beside the beanpole figure.

"I'm Willie," he heard the man say. "That's Jed here and that's Stiles on the horse." He snapped the reins and the wagon started forward as Janice included the three men in a quick smile.

"This is very good of you," she said, and Fargo grunted silently as he moved the Ovaro up until the horse's snout was almost inside the back opening of the Conestoga. His eyes peered into the wagon, halted at an open trunk to one side: an old, solid piece with heavy cast-iron fittings. His eyes roved across the contents and then moved on deeper into the wagon. A small pile of clothing had been pushed back against the sides of the wagon and he lingered on it for a moment, continued his slow survey of the inside of the wagon. He felt the muscle in his jaw throb as he slowed the Ovaro, drew back, moved up alongside the wagon.

The younger one with the two pearl-handled revolvers looked at him instantly as he moved the Ovaro forward, his stare cold, hostile. Fargo saw his hands rest on the butts of the two guns. The Ovaro moved forward, drew abreast of the driver's seat and a few paces ahead of the man on the horse. Fargo smiled as the sharp-faced man eyed him.

"Been thinking," he began mildly. "It's only right that I earn my pay. I decided I'll take the little lady on through myself."

He didn't have to see the protest leap into Janice's eyes. He knew it was there and he had more important things to do. It all erupted at once, as he knew it would. The young one on the horse started to draw the two pearl-handled revolvers. The balding one leaned back, reached inside the Conestoga, and brought out a rifle. The sharp-faced one held the horses steady.

But Fargo's big Colt exploded lead, shots fired so fast they almost seemed as one. He took the cold-eyed younger man on the horse first, and the two shots slammed into his midsection. The two pearl-handled revolvers flew into the air as the man clutched at his abdomen, doubled over, started to pitch forward out of the saddle.

Fargo had whirled the Colt, fired again. The balding one had brought the rifle around, on his feet and starting to aim. As Fargo's shots hit him, he became a strange dancer, twisting first one way, then the other, still clutching the rifle, his head thrown back as his chest gushed out red.

Janice was screaming in terror, but Fargo heard it only as a dim and distant sound, every fiber of his body, nerve, and mind concentrated on the split seconds between life and death. The sharp-faced man had dropped the reins, yanked an old Patterson Colt out, and almost got a shot off when the bullet plowed into the top of his forehead, made a deep furrow along the top of his head, sending up a shower of hair, blood, and bits of skull bone. He went backward, disappeared from sight, and Fargo heard his body hit the ground on the other side of the Conestoga.

Fargo drew a deep breath, blew on the barrel of the Colt. Janice was shaking violently, her face buried in her hands as she bent forward, head almost in her lap. "It's over," Fargo said. She didn't change position as she continued to shake.

He moved the Ovaro to the side of the wagon, reached out, pulled her hands from her face. She straighted, eyes wide, shock and terror still in their hazel depths as she stared at him. Slowly, the shock faded, the terror diminished, and he saw a kind of disbelief come into her eyes.

"You killed all of them," she breathed. "Just like that. You killed them."

He nodded. "Just like that," he echoed, holstered the Colt.

"All because they were going to be kind to me." She stared, the shock still in her eyes. "All because they were going to take me to Fort Kearny and you decided against it."

"They weren't going to take you to Fort Kearny," Fargo said as he swung down from the Ovaro. "They had other plans for you." Janice frowned, waited. "They were going to have themselves a high old time with you, honey," he said.

"You're just saying that," she countered.

He made a harsh sound. "They were going to screw you into the ground, honey, forwards, backwards, sideways, upside-down, and inside-out."

"You don't know anything of the sort," she protested.

"Take my word for it," he snapped.

"No, that's too easy for you, a quick way for you to justify what you did," Janice said. "I don't believe you."

"Honey, I don't give a damn whether you believe me or not," Fargo said. He untied her horse, tossed the reins to her, and climbed onto the wagon to drive it deep into a thicket of elms. He unhitched the horses, took their harnesses, bits, and bridles off, and let them run free. He walked back to where Janice stared at him with wariness, incomprehension still hanging in her stare.

"Three settlers out to make a new life for themselves," she said, her hazel eyes staring at him.

"Three pack rats. I did the world a favor," Fargo said.

Her hazel orbs were round as they stared back. "You tell yourself those things so you can sleep at night?" Janice said.

"I'll sleep just fine tonight," Fargo said. "Now let's move before we have more company we don't want."

He sent his horse into a trot and heard her follow. She hung back, her eyes still full of wariness, fear, shock, and disbelief. He rode out into open land, swore softly as his eyes scanned the ground. Indian pony tracks, too many, too old, and nothing else that might help. He cast a glance at Janice as she rode a safe distance back and watched him as though she wanted to see inside him. He ignored her, settled down to concentrate on signs, prints, markings, trails that might tell him what he wanted to know. But they told him little of value, and he swung the horse into the shade of a line of staghorn sumac as the sun began to blister the ground. He heard Janice call out suddenly, reined in the Ovaro.

"I have to stop. My leg has cramped up," she said. He watched her slide from the horse, put her weight on her left leg, and half-fall, half-hobble to a cluster of the staghorn sumacs to slump down against one. She made a face of pain as she tried to move her right leg, quickly stopped. "It's in my thigh," she said. "God, it hurts." Fargo brought the Ovaro closer, saw her eyes lift to him. "Could you just rub it for a minute?" she asked.

"A murderer like me?" he asked.

She looked back with her lips tightening against each other. "I can't ride this way," she muttered.

He dismounted, knelt down beside her, and she half-turned onto her side, gestured with one hand to the back of her left thigh. He put his hand on her, midway along the thigh, and rubbed gently. He felt no knotted muscles as she gasped in pain. He moved his hand farther up her thigh, closer to the round swell of her rear. She made no protest, and he moved his hand up again, almost to the full round curve. He could feel the heat of her through the skirt—nice, exciting, smooth. He pressed gently and still felt no knotted, cramped muscle. His hand rested just under the crease in her skirt where her round rear pulled the fabric in tight.

He saw her half-turn her torso, glanced up as her right arm came around, gathered speed. Too late, he saw the rock in her hand. He rolled, but the blow caught him alongside the temple and he fell on his side, rolled onto his stomach as purple and red and yellow lights danced in front of him. He felt the sudden weakness in his body, shook his head, started to pull himself around, saw dim outlines as she came down with the rock again, catching him atop the head this time. He pitched forward, no more flashing lights, no pain, only blackness. The world vanished, sense, feeling, all slipping away. He lay there, unmoving, unhearing, unseeing, and Janice Davidson stared down at him for a moment. Her hand opened and the rock fell from it, and she stood as if transfixed, trembled, wrenched herself around, and fled to where her horse waited. She sobbed as she leaped into the saddle, raced the horse away without glancing back. The edge of the woods grew silent, the swoop of a catbird the only movement.

Feeling returned first. Roughness, dirt pressed against his face, strangely welcome. Feeling meant life. He waited, let scent return, drew in the damp odor of soil close to his nostrils. He waited again and felt the throbbing of his head. Slowly he pulled eyelids open, the world fuzzy, everything indistinct. He pushed, rolled onto his back, forced eyelids open again, held them open until the world swam into focus, became sky, tree branches, leaves.

It all flew back into his thoughts with a quick sweep of memory, and he felt the rush of anger. "Bitch. Damn little bitch," he muttered as he pushed himself to his feet. His head throbbed and his temple ached. He whistled and the Ovaro trotted over, and he took his canteen, leaned against the horse as he opened it, doused his head with the cold water, waited, and did it again. The throbbing began to lessen and he patted his temple with his kerchief, saw that he had a bruise but the skin hadn't broken, and swore again. His eyes swept the loose, sandy soil and picked up the hoofprints of her horse at once. She'd gone south, he grunted, still bent on catching up to her pa. She'd been resentful, angry, stubborn, and the gunfight had turned it all into fear. He had grown stubborn himself at her attitude, figured she'd simmer down. A mistake, he saw now.

He shook his head, winced, and climbed onto the Ovaro. He'd have to go after the little fool, he swore silently, turned the horse onto the trail of hoofprints. He guessed she had an hour's head start, but the trail was fresh and clear, easy to follow.

She had struck out down the slope, across flat land at once, he saw. She'd enough sense not to race her horse, he noted, no deep, dug-in prints. He followed, had gone about a half-mile when he pulled up. Another set of her prints doubled back, swung away, headed for the trees to his right. She'd seen something, he grunted, enough to send her streaking for cover. Indian party, most likely.

He followed her trail as she reached the timber, kept going deep into the woods. She stayed there, turned south in the woodland, and he followed again when the terrain became drier and he was suddenly in a stretch of blackened, burned-out timberland, charred stumps standing like so many skeletons amid acres of fallen trees rising up in crazy angles. Lightning had plunged this section into a forest fire that had burned itself out. Not too recently, though, he noted, for the ground already carried a thin layer of vegetation, the soil full of life-giving humus, seedling taking root.

But the dried-out fallen trees and logs were an obstacle course. In more ways than one, he grunted. It was a perfect habitat for timber rattlers. He quickened the pinto's pace, taking the fallen trees in steady jumps, letting the ground resound to the horse's hooves. Rattlers would get out of the way, slide into cover, if you gave them a chance, most times. It was when you moved slowly, silently, came onto them unexpectedly that you brought trouble. He let the pinto take most of the jumps full out and knew the horse enjoyed it. The horse was a natural jumper, eager to meet the challenge of each jump with ears up, magnificent muscles gathered. He had just taken a pair of blackened logs piled atop each other when he caught the flash of pale yellow out of the corner of his eye, a sudden burst of brightness amid the gray and dark green.

He reined up, turned, and the pale yellow became ash-blond hair. He leaped from the saddle. She lay on her back beside a charred stump and he was beside her in three long strides. He saw the bruise on her left temple at once, caked blood, scraped skin, and beneath it, a lump already turning purple. He leaned down to her, listened to her long, shallow breaths. He looked up, swept the area with a quick glance. Her horse had fled. She'd been thrown, he knew. Perhaps taking a jump wrong. Or a rattler spooking her horse. But she'd been thrown, that much was plain, her temple hitting the edge of the charred stump.

He moved her head gently, felt along her collarbone and shoulders. Nothing broken, he muttered silently. He took his canteen, sprinkled some water on her, and she didn't respond. Damn, he swore, reached down, and gently lifted her limp form and draped her across his saddle. He walked to the horse's head, took the reins, and led the horse around fallen logs, past blackened, upended roots, carefully wending his way through the burned-out forest. He spotted two timber rattlers, gave each a wide berth. It was slow progress that used up time and nerves, and he was glad to see the fire-ravaged area came to an end in a wall of thick, green foliage.

He led the horse into the cool depths of the living woods and felt as though he had just passed through a vast graveyard. He looked back at Janice. Her limp form hung loosely across the saddle, ash-blond hair falling almost to the ground. He moved forward and caught the sound—bubbling water, a fast-moving brook—hurried on until he spied the bouncing, rippling thread of water, flashing in shafts of sunlight. He halted at the very edge, lifted Janice from the saddle, and put her down beside the brook.

Soaking his kerchief, he made it into a cold compress, bathed her temple, face, freshened the cloth, and laid it across her forehead. She didn't stir and he sat back, watching her with a frown, changing the compress every few minutes. He had almost decided he'd have to try to get her a doctor when he saw the blond eyelashes flutter. He moved the compress from her forehead and her eyes half-opened, closed again. A small sound came from her, became almost a moan, and he watched the blond eyelashes flutter again, close, and she fell silent.

He waited, watching, frowned in concern, and suddenly her eyes opened, stared, unfocused. He reached over, pressed a hand gently at the back of her neck. Slowly her eyes changed, their hazel depths taking on comprehension as the vacant stare drifted away.

She turned her head, saw him, blinked, and he watched the mixture of relief and chagrin come into her eyes. She pushed herself onto her elbows and winced in pain. "Horse threw me," she murmured. "Spooked at something."

"Rattler, probably," Fargo said. She sat up straighter and winced again. "Easy," Fargo said, and handed her the cold, wet kerchief. "Put this on again for a few minutes," he said.

She lay back and put the compress over her forehead. "I just took a bad fall," she said.

"More than that. Mild concussion, I'd guess. You've been out a long time," Fargo said. She lay still as he got to his feet, his eyes sweeping the trees. "You see which way your horse went?" he asked.

She shook her head as she sat up and handed him the kerchief. "No," she answered.

He wrung the kerchief out over the brook, his lips tight. "Got to find him," he said.

"I'll walk," Janice said.

He tossed her a hard glance. "With a horse you're just a pain in the ass. Without one, you're a damn liability," he snapped. "We've got to find your horse."

He saw the hazel eyes grow copper at once. "You can always shoot me, too," she said waspishly. "Then I wouldn't be a problem."

His face stayed as if carved in stone. "It's a thought," he said, and saw the flash of fright touch her eyes before she looked away. He pulled himself onto the Ovaro. "Get up here," he said, and she obeyed with her lips drawn in crossly, sat the saddle in front of him. He reached around her and took the reins, and his arms pressed against the soft sides of her breasts. She tried to shift but there was no place to go. He shifted his weight in the saddle and knew she felt him pressing against the soft curve of the end of her spine.

He smiled, sent the Ovaro into a trot, and the motion rubbed his dormant but nonetheless thick, heavy organ up and down against her. He felt her try to hold herself away from him, but it was an impossible task with the horse at a trot.

"Couldn't we go slower? My head still bothers me," she said.

"Just your head?" he said as he slowed the horse. She didn't answer and he knew she heard his soft laugh. He enjoyed the soft warmth of her against him and concentrated on picking up trail marks before his dormant organ stirred itself into eagerness.

Her horse had gone deeper through the woods, turned, broke off a half-dozen low twigs as he pushed through the dense foliage. "What made you double back into the trees?" Fargo asked.

Janice turned in the saddle to look at him and he saw the surprise in her eyes.

"You didn't think I came onto you by luck, did you?" he pushed at her.

"No, I suppose not," she muttered. "A line of

Indians came over a hill and I ran before they saw me."

"You were lucky," he said, his eyes searching out more signs. The trees grew less densely packed and the horse had gone on in a more or less straight line. A row of stomped on horse mushrooms marked his path and Fargo followed until he suddenly reined up.

"What is it?" Janice asked, eyes wide.

He put a hand over her mouth. "I smell bear grease," he whispered. He slid from the saddle, landed on the tips of his toes to move forward in a crouch. He saw her swing to the ground to follow and he rested behind a row of ebony spleenwort, bracken, and wild clover. She came up to drop down beside him. "Somebody found your horse," he whispered, and she followed his gaze to where the two Indians sat in the woods. They sat cross-legged and were intent on devouring a cluster of wild strawberries. Janice's big dark bay stood tied to the Indian ponies a few paces away.

"Crow," Fargo whispered, taking in the design on the anklet one wore. The other was naked, save for his breechclout, a thin-framed figure, almost skeletal, long, black hair heavy with bear grease. The one with the anklet was shorter, stocky, with something of a roll of fat around his middle.

"You going to pick them off?" Janice whispered.

He shook his head. "No shots if I can help it. Might bring others down on us."

She watched him draw the thin, double-edged throwing knife from its holster around his calf. He dropped to his stomach. "You stay here. Don't move, don't make any noise," he said. "And stay down." She nodded and he waited until she stretched out on her stomach. He started to crawl forward then, edging his way, silent as a diamondback approaching its prey. He crept closer and the two Crow stayed intent on gorging themselves with the fruit. The thin blade in his hand, he risked inching a few feet closer, halted, pushed himself up on one hand, and started to draw his arm back. He chose the thin-framed one and took aim. The sound came from behind him—a sneeze, but it sounded as though a shotgun had gone off in the stillness.

"Shit!" Fargo swore as the two Crow leaped to their feet as if on springs. He pulled his arm back. He couldn't throw the blade now. The two Crow were moving, every sense alerted, their eyes peering into the foliage. Surprise had vanished with the sneeze. The thin one motioned and they spread apart, drew tomahawks and started toward him, eyes narrowed as they scanned the trees.

Fargo waited a second longer. He'd lost the advantage of surprise and he'd have to get it back. The two Crow hadn't drawn a fix on him yet, but they were coming close to it as they sniffed and searched. Fargo tucked the thin blade up into his sleeve, held it in place with his hand cupped, and sprang up, catapulting himself into full view of the two Crow. They froze for an instant, startled, then charged at him. He turned, ran straight to his left, threw a quick glance back. The thin-bodied one was first after him, darting through the trees.

Fargo let himself look scared. It didn't take much acting, he grunted silently, turned, and ran on. He slowed a few paces on, threw another glance back to see the thin-framed Indian fling his tomahawk on the run. The short-handled ax hurtled through the air with deadly accuracy, and Fargo dropped to a crouch, felt the tomahawk graze his hair as it slammed into the tree just behind him. He started to run again, the Indian racing after him. Fargo halted and spun as he let the throwing knife drop from his sleeve into his hand. He flung the blade, a quick, upward motion.

The Crow, charging hard, was unable to change direction and met the blade in midair as it pierced his naked abdomen, burying itself up to the hilt. He stumbled forward, fell to his knees, surprise and anguish in his broad-cheeked face. He clutched at the hilt of the blade with both hands in a vain effort to pull it free, but it had gone in too deeply and he made a gargling noise, pitched forward to lie on his face, a last twitching spasm moving his legs.

Fargo had gone into a half-crouch as the other Crow came toward him, the tomahawk in his right hand. The Indian circled and Fargo circled with him, stepped forward, and saw the Crow's arm muscles tighten, the tomahawk start to move forward. Fargo halted and the Indian pulled back, waited, his stocky frame circling again. Fargo moved with him once again, his mouth a hard, thin line. He had to test the Crow's speed. He came in, feinted, started a charge. The Crow swung downward with the tomahawk and Fargo drew back, easily avoiding the blow, and kept the smile inside himself. The Crow's ample midsection made him slow.

Fargo stepped backward and let the Indian come at him, waited, feinted again, and the Crow swung the tomahawk in a flat arc. Fargo timed his pull-back and the ax whistled past his chin. His right came down over the Indian's brow, caught the Crow alongside the face, and the Indian half-fell sideways, started to turn, but Fargo's left whistled upward, all his strength behind it. He drove the blow at the point of the Indian's jaw and the man spun, fell backward, the tomahawk dropping from his hand. He rolled, reached for it, but Fargo's big hand closed around it first. The Crow found the strength to leap upward, hands outstretched toward his foe's throat. Fargo brought the tomahawk around in a powerful backhanded blow. The edge of the weapon caught the Crow across the side of the neck, severing tendons, muscles, arteries. He crumpled as the life ran out of him and Fargo stepped back, dropped the tomahawk on the ground beside him.

He had just retrieved his throwing knife and wiped it clean in the grass when he saw Janice stand up, move toward him. His glare fastened on her. "Jesus," he spit out.

"A piece of grass got into my nose," she said.

"You're getting to be a damn menace," Fargo growled. "You almost got us both killed."

"I couldn't help it. I'm sorry," she said with a defensive anger.

"Sorry's only good for your conscience," he snapped. "Get your horse."

He watched her pick her way around the two still figures, untie the bay, and climb onto the horse. He was astride the Ovaro when she rode up, his eyes frosted blue. "You better get something straight, honey," he said. "You do a boneheaded thing like that again and I'll leave you to get yourself killed."

Her hazel eyes peered hard at him. "Why didn't you this time? Why'd you come after me?" she asked.

"I made a deal to get you to Fort Kearny," he said.

Her blond eyebrows knitted together. "I don't understand you," she said.

"You don't have to understand me. You just have to pay attention," he growled. "Let's ride. There's just enough day left to find a safe spot for the night."

5

Fargo set off, moving toward the edge of the timberland, and Janice rode a half-dozen lengths behind him. He found a glen with slab rock on one side and slid from his horse just as night slipped over the land. Janice had put out her bedroll, undressed in the dark of the bushes again, returned in the long, red cotton nightdress. The moon had grown stronger and he had laid out some beef jerky. She ate in silence and settled down on her bedroll. He felt her eyes on him as he laid out his own bedroll, started to unbutton his shirt.

"I suppose you think I ought to be grateful," she slid at him.

"Didn't think you knew the word," Fargo commented.

"I am grateful," Janice said, "but that doesn't change anything about your gunning down those three settlers."

He peered through the dim moonlight that had come up and his voice was harsh. "Come morning, I'm going to do something for you," he said. "I'm going to do it just this once. There won't be a second time no matter what you think."

He finished unbuttoning his shirt, slipped it off, stripped down his pants, and knew she watched him. He stretched, flexed tight leg and shoulder muscles.

"I suppose you think I ought to be grateful that you keep your underpants on," he heard her mutter.

"Nope. I figure you ought to be disappointed," he said.

He heard a hiss of exasperation as she flounced around on the bedroll, turned her back to him. He lay down, irritation hanging on. The day had been wasted chasing after her, time he'd have to make up somehow. A visit to Sam Rawley seemed unavoidable now. He let sleep wash over him, welcomed its peace, and the night passed quietly.

He woke first and felt the irritation still pulling at him as he glanced at Janice's sleeping form. As she slept, the dark-red nightdress had rolled up to midthigh on one leg, revealing a long, lovely calf, a slender thigh, a nicely rounded knee, all a creamy white. She woke suddenly, snapped eyes open, and grew angry at once as she pushed the nightdress down and glared at him.

"I suppose looking away would have been too much to expect," she sniffed as she got to her feet.

"Now why would I do that?" he answered.

"Good manners," she threw back.

"Good manners is one thing. Being dumb's another," he said. "Move your ass. We've a lot of ground to backtrack."

She stalked into the bushes and he had finished saddling the Ovaro when she returned, wearing a pale-blue sleeveless shirt that stretched downward tight over her breasts. He saw not the tiniest point in the fabric where it pulled taut, not even the darker coloration of nipples through the garment; he grunted to himself and swung onto his horse, started out of the glen.

She followed a few paces behind and he headed back the way they had come. Because he had to go back to find Sam Rawley's spread, the trip wouldn't be an entire waste, but he steered a wide circle around the edge of the burned-out area. The long way was better than the rattler-infested, obstacle-filled section, he decided.

He halted once to let the horses drink from a stream. Janice had ridden in silence most of the morning, but her eyes sought his as the horses refreshed themselves. "What is this that you're going to do for me?" she asked, sarcasm heavy in her voice.

"Teach you a damn lesson," Fargo said. "Maybe open your eyes some. Or maybe just waste my time." He saw the wariness come into the hazel eyes as he moved the Ovaro across the stream and went on.

She followed, rode beside him, her face set. He watched her as she rode, decided that the sleeveless shirt made her seem slenderer, more fragile. A deception, he grunted, recalling the way she'd used the rock on him. The trip ate away at the day and it was long past the noon hour when he reached the place where he'd pushed the wagon deep into the trees.

He dismounted, walked to the wagon, and Janice followed to where he halted at the tail end of the Conestoga. She questioned with her eyes and he gestured to the old trunk he had seen inside the wagon. "Look inside . . . that book there on top," he said.

Janice reached into the trunk, pulled the book out, and stared down at it in her hands. "The Holy Bible," she said.

"That's what it is," Fargo said. "Can you see any

of those three rotten-mouthed bastards carrying the Bible?"

She looked at him, frowned, opened the book to the first page. "This bible is given to Hannah Martins on her tenth birthday," she read, paused, glanced at Fargo with her lips tight. She tilted the Bible accidentally and a piece of paper fluttered out from the inside pages. She bent down, picked it up, stared at it. " 'On this day of October twelve, eighteen forty-one, Hannah Martins and Joseph Groh have been married before me and in the presence of witnesses and the sight of Our Lord. George Rivers, Justice of the Peace,' " Janice read.

She put the certificate into the Bible, closed the book, returned it to the trunk. "Look back of the trunk, at the space along the side of the wagon," Fargo said.

She peered in, stared at the clothes stuffed into the space. "Woman's bonnet, dress, purse," she murmured, turned around to look at Fargo, her eyes wide. "What happened to Hannah and Joseph?" she asked.

He shrugged.

"Are you saying those three men took the wagon, killed Hannah and Joseph Groh?" she asked.

"Maybe not. More likely Indians killed them and those three came along later, found the wagon, and took it for themselves," Fargo said.

She stared at the big man, tried to see behind the lake-blue eyes and the chiseled handsomeness. "How did you know? About them?" she asked. "You saw the Bible and grew suspicious?"

"I knew before that. The Bible and the women's clothes only nailed it down," Fargo said.

"How did you know?" she asked again.

"Some trails are in the grass, some are in a man's

face," he told her. "Those three read as small-time hustlers. Settlers don't sport two pearl-handled pistols. That one fancied himself a gunslinger. No good, none of them."

Her eyes studied him. "You're a strange one," she said. "You carry your own strange set of values. You thought nothing of killing those three men, but you're bent on stopping a massacre."

"Some killing's deserved, some isn't," he said.

"You broke your promise to my father, yet you came after me to keep it," Janice said. "I don't understand you."

"I told you, no need to understand, just listen. I said they were no good. I'm not proving anything else to you," he growled.

"You could have explained more," she muttered.

"You could've believed more," he countered, and walked back to the Ovaro, pulled himself onto the horse.

She followed, her face almost contrite. "What now?" she asked.

"Find a man named Sam Rawley and pay him a visit," Fargo said as he moved the horse forward down a long hill with only a few clusters of bur oak to break the expanse of fescue grasses. He turned at the bottom, led the way up another hill, less long, and he had crested the top. His eyes sweeping the land below, he saw the wagon at once. A cut-under runabout, a girl driving the horse hard, and he quickly saw the reason as he spotted the four bucks halfway up the side of the hill, chasing the runabout and starting to swing down toward it.

Janice came up and her eyes widened in fright. He took the bay by the cheek strap, pulled the horse back below the crest of the hill. He swung from the Ovaro in one graceful motion. "Get down and stay down," he barked at Janice as he drew the big Sharps rifle from its saddle case, shoved extra ammunition into his pocket, and dropped to the ground, crawled the few feet back to the crest of the hill.

The four bucks had closed ground, were starting to swing in on her tail as the girl whipped the horse with the reins, raced the runabout in a straight line. Fargo began firing the big Sharps, not aiming, sending a volley of shots that bracketed the four charging bucks. He reloaded, fired again, fired the Colt with his left hand as he reloaded the Sharps again. No aiming, no lone marksman shooting that would alert the Crow to the fact there was but one rifleman. He fired shots as fast as he could, letting bullets hit brush, dirt, rock, and he saw it was working as the four bucks reined up, wheeled their ponies, milled around for a moment. He let go another volley and saw the four Indians gather direction, race their ponies up the far hill, certain they were being attacked by a sizable force.

Fargo waited, gave the four red men plenty of chance to put time and distance between them before standing up on the crest. He brought the Ovaro up slowly, mounted, and started down to where the girl had halted the runabout. Her eyes were on him as he rode down the hill, dark-brown eyes, he saw, and long brown hair, almost a snub nose over a wide mouth with very full lips, a face that held no distinctive features yet pulled itself together to be attractive enough. Perspiration had soaked the front of her blouse and twin little points pushed into the fabric at the tips of small, upturned breasts.

"Where are the others?" she said, her breath still coming hard, he saw, and her eyes focused beyond his figure.

"No others. I put on an act that worked," he said. He saw her eyes stay fixed past him, half-turned in the saddle to see Janice moving slowly down the hill on the bay. "She's with me," he said.

The girl brought her eyes back to him and he saw her take in his chiseled face, move across the power in his chest and arms. She drew a deep breath, shook her head, as if suddenly realizing it was over. "God, I thought I was done for," she said.

He moved the Ovaro alongside the runabout, peered hard at her as she rubbed a hand across her face. "You all right?" he asked.

She nodded, drew another breath. "Yes," she said. "Quite all right now. I'm Vicky Benton," Her eyes met his, filled with a sudden rush of warmth. "Thanks isn't much of a word, sometimes," she said.

"It'll do," he answered as Janice came up. He saw not only curiosity in Vicky Benton's quick glance at her but a very female recognition of Janice's striking, blond loveliness.

"Janice Davidson," he introduced. "Vicky Benton."

Janice's half-smile held coolness; Vicky's quick smile was made of warmth.

"I was very lucky you were both riding by," Vicky said.

"*He* was riding by," Janice corrected.

Fargo's eyes snapped up to the top of the hill behind the runabout and the Colt was in his hand before the two young women heard the sound of the horses. His eyes were narrowed on the hilltop as the two riders came over it, one wearing a tan stetson, the other hatless, thinning gray hair blowing wildly.

"My father and Hank Thorst," Vicky Benton said, and he caught the flatness that had come into her voice. He saw her pleasantly attractive face set itself, as though she were bracing herself. Her father turned out to be the hatless one as he raced his horse to a skidding halt beside the wagon. Fargo saw a wiry-framed man, a narrow face with very intense, almost-burning blue eyes.

"You goddamn fool girl," the man roared at his daughter. "How many times I tell you not to go ridin' out alone? I came lookin' for you when I heard the shooting."

Fargo cut into the man's wrath. "Four bucks were chasing her. I managed to scare them off," he said.

"He was wonderful," Vicky said. "I thought a posse had come up."

The man's intense eyes turned to Fargo. "Much obliged to you, mister. I'm Tom Benton," he said.

"Skye Fargo," the big man replied.

Tom Benton's intense eyes widened in surprise. "Fargo? The Trailsman?" Skye nodded. "You're the feller Major Keyser told me he sent out. He told me all about it." The man's eyes went to Janice. "Didn't say anything about a gal, though," he added.

Fargo heard the ice form on Janice's words. "No, I'm one of Fargo's afterthoughts," she said tartly.

Fargo saw Vicky Benton's brows knit in a hint of a frown. "Jance is Colonel Davidson's daughter. She'll be riding with me till I can get her to Fort Kearny," he explained.

"Hardly my choice," Janice snapped out, and Fargo saw curiosity in Vicky Benton's eyes as they held on Janice.

"I'm looking for Sam Rawley's place," Fargo said.

"I can tell you where that is," Tom Benton said, saw Fargo's eyes go to the man beside him, tall, hard gray-blue eyes, a thin mouth, and a long jaw. "Sorry, this is Hank Thorst. Hank works with me," the man introduced. "Look, it'll be dark soon. You can visit Sam Rawley come morning. Come to my place for the night. I owe you a dinner and more for saving my damn-fool daughter's hide."

Fargo watched Vicky flare at once. "Your damn-fool daughter wouldn't be out here if it weren't for you," she flung back, snapped the reins, and wheeled the runabout in a tight circle.

"Rotten temper," Tom Benton said. "Comes from having too much female upbringing. Now you and Miss Janice here just come along and spend the night, and we can talk over a good square meal." His intense blue eyes turned to Janice. "I'm sure this young lady could stand a real bed for the night, even a hard one," he added.

"That would be indeed welcome," Janice accepted quickly.

"Then it's settled," Tom Benton said, turned his horse, and started to follow the runabout as Vicky had already started to drive away. Hank Thorst fell in beside him, and Fargo shrugged, followed the two men with Janice at his side. She radiated a kind of smugness and his glance at her was hard.

"Don't get any ideas," Fargo murmured.

She looked at him innocently. "I can't think what you're talking about," she said.

"Hell you can't," Fargo growled. "Don't figure to stay on with Benton and then take off on your own while I'm out scouting."

"I just look forward to a good night's sleep in a real bed," she said.

Fargo's grunt was filled with skepticism. "Keep it at that," he said.

They had moved onto flat prairie land. Fargo's eyes were on Vicky as she drove the runabout a dozen yards ahead when Tom Benton seemed to explode in a fit of coughing. He halted his horse, doubled over in the saddle with the sudden attack of hard, hacking coughs that convulsed his wiry frame and made his thinning gray hair bounce up and down.

Fargo saw Vicky halt the runabout and look back, the frown of concern wreathing her face. The other man sat patiently, not moving, as Tom Benton continued to cough in harsh spasms. Fargo listened to the sound, the dry, tight, racking coughing that spelled lung problems, and Tom Benton finally stopped, drew in deep gasping breaths, and moved his horse forward. Fargo followed, saw Janice frowning.

"Tuberculosis?" she whispered to Fargo.

He shrugged. "Maybe. Maybe not. All kinds of ways to get bad lungs," he said.

Janice fell silent again as they rode on in the fading light of the late afternoon. The house came into view, finally, and Fargo felt surprise dig at him as he took in a frame structure that sagged at one end, part of the side weathered, cracked wood, a small barn near that sported only half a roof. Vicky drove the cut-under runabout into the barn as Fargo halted before the house.

"I'll bet getting on," Thorst said to Tom Benton.

The man nodded. "You know what to do," he answered, and the hard-faced man nodded to the others, unsmiling, rode away at a fast trot. Tom Benton's intense blue eyes turned on Janice and his half-bow held a kind of formal gallantry in it. "This way, Miss Janice," he said. "Got some fine sherry inside."

"Wonderful," Janice said, and accompanied him into the house, the door hanging on one hinge, Fargo noted. He waited as Vicky emerged from the barn, walked toward him, her perspiration-soaked blouse resting on the tiny, sharp tips almost caressingly. Her dark-brown eyes looked up at him and she followed with an engaging smile.

"Sorry about flaring up back there," she said.

"No need to be sorry to me," Fargo said.

"Still bad manners, losing my temper when I could've lost my life, except for you," she said. Her hand came out, pressed his arm, a sudden, impulsive gesture full of warmth. "Thanks is still a small word," she said. "Maybe I can find something better." She didn't look away from his appraising stare.

"Work on it," he said, smiling slowly.

She nodded, halted as they reached the doorway. "Would you be staying on after this is over, if there's anyone left?" she asked, sudden bitterness coming into her voice.

"Not likely, 'less I had a special reason," he said.

Her quick smile was bright. "Maybe I can find one for you," she said, went into the house, and he watched her rear move under the skirt. Nice, tight, neat, he murmured inwardly. "I'll join you soon as I change out of this blouse," she said, hurried on.

Fargo found himself in a front room with barewood walls, cracked panels, a stone fireplace at one end with the corner stones crumbled. He saw more rooms leading off beyond it. Janice was seated on a hide-covered stool beside a warped table, a tin mug in one hand. Tom Benton sat on a straight-backed chair across from her. "Come in," the man called. "Miss Janice and I've been talking about Kansas. Spent some time back there when I was a young man. Drink? I've some good whiskey."

"That'd be fine," Fargo said, and Tom Benton gestured to a two-seat stuffed settee with the fabric worn raw. Fargo eased himself onto the piece, fearful whether it would collapse under him. But it was sturdy enough and the man brought him a shot glass of whiskey. Fargo took a pull on it and decided that Tom Benton knew little about good whiskey.

"Vicky's had a stew cooking all afternoon. Be about ready now," the man said, and his blue eyes seemed to never lose their intensity, as though they were fired by some inner tension. He began to cough but only a few hard, hacking sounds this time, and he downed the contents of the tin mug in his hand. "Sherry. Helps warm the insides," the man murmured.

Vicky came into the room, included everyone in a quick, bright smile that rested longest on the big black-haired man with the lake-blue eyes. Her small, sharp breasts still turned upward saucily in the white, crisp blouse she had changed into, Fargo noted. She went to the fireplace, started to pull the heavy black kettle simmering over the embers.

Fargo rose. "I'll get that for you," he said. He took the iron hook from her, lifted the pot onto a small stone stand to the right of the crumbling fireplace stones. Standing against her, he caught the faint fragrance of the perfume she'd put on, a dusky, sensuous odor. He stepped back as Tom Benton came over with four tin plates.

"Good food tastes good no matter what you eat it on," the man said.

"It tastes better on good plates," Vicky snapped, and again Fargo caught the quick-tempered annoyance at her father. The man ignored her comment, pushed chairs to the table, and Janice pulled her hide-covered stool over. Fargo sat down opposite the man, beside Janice, felt Tom Benton's intense eyes on him.

"You got a lead on anything so far, Fargo?" the man asked.

"Managed to break up one attack on a Crow camp, but no leads," Fargo answered as Janice put a plate of the stew before him.

"Got any ideas on what to do?" the man asked. "You can't cover the whole territory by yourself."

"Don't have to. Whoever's behind it has to concentrate around where the small Indian camps are set up," Fargo returned.

"That's true," Tom Benton agreed thoughtfully. "But that's still pretty much a hit-and-miss chore."

"That's why I want to visit this Sam Rawley. You know that Major Keyser figures he's the one behind stirring the tribes up," Fargo said.

"I know it. The major talked about it with me," Tom Benton said, and Fargo watched Vicky sit down with her plate after serving everyone else. Janice dug into her food with relish. Vicky ate with small, thoughtful bites, he noticed.

"Talk about this bother you, Vicky?" he asked.

She nodded vigorously. "The whole thing bothers me," she said. "But go on. Not talking about it won't make it go away."

Fargo returned his attention to her father. "You agree with the major's thinking?" he asked.

"Got to agree with it," the man said. "Sam Rawley's a hard man, doesn't care about anyone or anything except himself. He's got the land fever to push him on and the manpower to make it work. I just don't think you've enough time left to prove it." He halted and his face flushed. The coughing followed at once, shook his body violently, but ended sooner than when he'd been on the horse. "Sorry," he said when his breath returned. "As you can guess, I came out here for my health, lung problems."

"It hasn't helped any," Fargo heard Vicky cut in, glanced at her to see she was staring at her plate, her face tight.

"Vicky's impatient," her father said. "Been trying to set up a little income-producing business, but it looks as if I'm going to have to leave everything if I want to keep my skin. Stayed this long hoping things would simmer down, but it doesn't seem like it will."

Vicky's voice cut in again and Fargo saw her eyes on him. "I'll take you to see Sam Rawley in the morning," she said. "You can make up a reason for the visit, I'm sure."

"You've a deal," Fargo said.

"If he's the one behind it and you can stop him, I want to help," she said, rising and collecting the plates, her face still tight. She moved with quick, almost-angry motions, and the sharp tiny nipples pushed themselves into the white blouse, her small breasts jiggling provocatively.

Tom Benton stretched. "I'm an early-to-bed, early-to-rise type," he announced. "So if you'll excuse me, I'll see you come morning." He turned to Janice. "Take the last room on this side of the house. It has a few cracks in the walls, but it's a warm night and it has the best bed."

"Thank you, Tom. I'll be fine, I know," she said, and Vicky's father walked from the room, disappeared into one of the other rooms, and Fargo heard him wrestle with a door that moved in protest.

Janice rose. "I'm exhausted myself, I'll turn in, too," she said.

"I'll get you a fresh candle," Vicky said, rising to take a short, fat hard-wax, hand-dipped candle from a box on the floor. She secured it to a round, small iron candleholder and lit it, handed it to Janice.

Fargo took in the two young women as they stood almost side by side. Direct contrasts, he grunted, with each other and with themselves: Janice, a full, ripe body, soft, swelling, smoothly round breasts, full womanly thighs; Vicky, small-breasted, saucy, a wiry sensuousness to her—Janice, all blond; Vicky dark—the full-breasted, ripe Janice, delicate and held-back; the small, saucy Vicky, sensuous and pulsating.

Vicky saw Janice down the hallway to the last room and Fargo rose, went to the open doorway of the house where it hung askew from its one hinge. He stepped outside, listened to the night sounds under a bright half-moon. The prairie stretched flat and the distant cry of coyotes drifted to him and he caught the swooping flight of brown bats silhouetted against the moon. A small cluster of black locust trees were a dark bulk a few dozen yards from the house.

Vicky appeared silently at his side. "Let's walk some," she said. She headed toward the trees and he walked beside her, felt the darkness of her mood.

"What's bothering you?" he asked.

"This place, all we're facing, everything," she said.

"Your pa?" he added.

"Yes," she said, cast a quick glance up at him. "I came here because he begged me to nurse him, cook for him, take care of him. No question that he was sick and needed help, and I agreed. He told me he had this fine house." She paused and her laugh was harsh with bitterness. "You saw it, that broken-down wreck of a place," she said.

"Why'd he lie to you?" Fargo asked.

"He needed someone to nurse him back to health,

and he was afraid I might refuse. We've been here near a year now and I can't see him getting any better. But he keeps saying he has to go on a little longer," Vicky said.

"Go on for what?" Fargo questioned.

"The business. Hank Thorst is supposed to be getting customers for a freight service. Pa's backing him, sends him off every week, but I don't see any customers. Maybe because there aren't any out here in this godforsaken place," she said, drew a deep breath. "I don't want to talk about it," she said, halting under the trees and looking up at him. "You're the only good thing that's come this way since I've been here. Not just because you saved my skin," she said.

"What, then?" Fargo asked.

Her arms reached up, encircled his neck, pulled his face down to hers, and her lips pressed hard against his. "This," she said.

"Being grateful for this afternoon?" Fargo asked.

"No, just being hungry," Vicky answered, and he liked the direct honesty of her. She opened her lips again, waited for him this time, and he kissed her, felt the sweet softness of her lips, let his tongue reach out, explore, probe.

Vicky shuddered, pushed her own tongue forward, darting little motions, then quick, almost-savage thrustings. He sank down on the grass, pulled her with him, his hand reaching into the neck of the blouse.

"Oh, Jesus, oh, God, Fargo," she gasped as his hand pressed against one saucy breast under the blouse. She wriggled and the blouse came off. Her breasts, free of the blouse, remained small but beautifully perky, curving upward from the undersides to thrust up and forward, nipples taut, pointing upward, pink-brown with small areolas of matching color. They seemed almost to quiver in eagerness, flesh reflecting spirit, and he bent down, sucked one hard little tip into his mouth. Vicky half-screamed, pressed forward, pushed all of the small breast into his mouth.

He slid out of clothes as he caressed the breast with his tongue, pulled gently on it, and she screamed in joy, a sudden, sharp sound. Her hand pushed at the top of her skirt and the garment slid down until she kicked it free. She lay back for him—slender hips, almost bony; legs almost thin—her body, like the features of her face, were undistinguished separately, yet together, it made an attractive little package. A rounded little belly was unexpectedly sensuous, as was the very bushy, very black little mound just beneath it.

He cupped one saucy upturned breast with his hand, stroked the hard little nipple with his thumb, and felt her hips move upward at once. She reached one arm up, circled his neck, pulled him down to her breast, offering, pleading, and he drew the little mound into his mouth.

"Jesus . . . aaaaah, ah, Jesus, oh, please, oh . . . oh," she murmured, gasped words as she quivered, writhed, pushed upward with her breast, and he felt the hard little tip press against the roof of his mouth. Her hands moved up and down his body, along his ribs, pressed hard, clasped around his back. Vicky Benton pulled at him, her legs falling open, and her words were hardly more than throaty sounds. "Please . . . ah . . . please . . . yes . . . yes . . . oh, God, yes."

He brought his powerful body over hers and she

felt suddenly very small, his eager, pulsing organ pressed into her round little belly. "Oooooh, oh, Fargo . . . oh, my God," she half-screamed, pushed herself upward along the grass, then down, trying to take him in, the lock seeking the key.

He moved for her, let the very tip of his throbbing, wet shaft rest at the edge of her warm lips, and her scream was full-throated this time, wanting, needing, frantic, thirsting desire part of her cry. She thrust herself upward and forward over him, legs locking tight behind his back. "Eeeeeee . . . oh, agh . . . aaaah," she moaned, and in the sound there was more than desire, more than welcome, a kind of overwhelming relief. He moved in her, slowly, and she sobbed out little moans in rhythm, her hips lifting up with his every tantalizing movement. She held him with her inner walls, warm, wet, encompassing, and her hands cupped her breasts, pushed them upward for him, offering, entreating. He took first one, then the other, and her hands went to his body again, dug in, clasped themselves around his buttocks, and pressed, fingers digging into his skin as if she could claw her way into his very innards.

He felt her suddenly stiffen, legs locked behind his back came unlocked, stretch out, and her hands grew into little fists. "Coming," she gasped. "Coming . . . coming, oh, Jesus, Jesus, Jesus. . . ." He moved hard inside her, deep, deeper, quickened his thrusts as she hissed out little sounds. Her slender body seemed to gather new strength, arched itself backward, the saucy little upturned breasts quivering. Her scream spiraled, circled, hung in the air, finally died away as a long, breathy gasp. He pressed his face over one beautiful little breast and the pink-brown tip rested in the corner of his eye. Finally he rolled onto his back, took her with him, and she straddled him as she fell forward over his chest.

"Oh, God, Fargo . . . oh, God. It's been so damn long," Vicky Benton breathed. She stayed astride him, holding him inside her. He stroked her body with both hands, felt the small protrusions of her spine rise from her thin back. "I never threw it around, but back home there were a few men, at least. I've been shriveling up here, turning everything inside myself. I've been almost glad the Indians are taking the warpath. We'll have to leave here then," she said.

"Where's back home?" he asked as she seemed perfectly content to hold him inside her as she talked.

"Arkansas," she said. "Pa and my ma split a long time ago and Ma raised me. He used to send money every month, though. Then three years ago he stopped, just seemed to disappear. It was then that Ma got sick and died. I stayed on and a little over a year ago he showed up, coughing and sick."

"That's when he asked you to come out here with him," Fargo said, and she nodded, moved, slid herself from him finally. He turned and she rolled onto her back and he admired the pert turn of the small breasts that seemed forever eager in their upward curving loveliness.

"Dammit, Fargo, why do you have to get her to Fort Kearny? Why not stay here?" Vicky Benton said in a rush of petulance.

"Her old man's paid me to get her there," he said.

She sniffed. "That's all the pay you'll get," she said. "She won't be giving you anything."

He laughed. "Wishful thinking or instinct?" he asked.

"Both," she said, and her smile was quick, full of brightness.

"Maybe I'll circle back after," he said.

"Would you?" she squealed at once.

"Why not?" he answered. "But you said it yourself, that depends on whether all hell breaks loose."

She grew silent, her face darkening at once, turned, lifted herself over his chest. Her lips found his, pressed, pushed his mouth open, and her tongue rushed forward, quivered, caressed, drew back. "Now is here. Tomorrow's a maybe," she said, and her hand moved down his chest, across his flat, hard abdomen, found his waiting maleness already surging, expanding. She pressed fingers around him, stroked, flung herself from his chest, and pressed her face against the throbbingness of him, made tiny little sounds as she drew him into her lips, caressed, pulled, broke off suddenly to fling her hips over him, ram herself onto him.

Vicky Benton pumped, pushed, drew back, rammed down again, and her breath came in tiny puffing spurts until she flung herself onto his chest, arms around the back of his neck, and he rolled with her, took her again, heard her scream of ecstasy as she came for him and he stayed in her, still pulsing, still ready.

"Too quick, too quick," she breathed angrily at herself.

He moved inside her, slowly now, and she cried out, sucked in breath, held for a moment, then responded, pushed against him. "Easy, now," he

94

murmured, and she nodded against his cheek. But the body denied too long is its own mistress, and he felt her pelvis surging, harder, faster. He stayed with a slow rhythm as long as he could, held her back, but her head tossed from side to side in frenzy, her hands digging into him again.

"Please, please, please," she cried out. "Oh, God, oh, oh, oh, Jesus, Fargo . . . please." He drew back and pushed hard, deep. "Aaaaah, ah, yes, yes, ah, ah . . . ah," she begged, and he let himself come with her as she stiffened again, arched, lifted, and clung to that cresting moment, eternal ecstasy, the promise fulfilled that vanished so quickly.

She moaned little sounds finally as she lay under him, her body limp but her arms clinging to him, holding his powerful chest pressed against her breasts. He stayed unmoving until her arms fell away, a gesture almost of defeat, an admittance that ecstasy was beyond capture.

He lay beside her and let the night breeze cool the heat of his body, finally pushed onto his elbows, looked down at her.

She opened her eyes, the quick smile holding satisfied smugness in it. The moon was far down the blue-black corridor in the sky, and she read his eyes, pulled herself up. "You made all the waiting worth it, Fargo," she said. She stood up, again seemed much smaller, slenderer naked than in clothes, and she was dressed before he finished, her hands rubbing his chest as he put his shirt on. "I'm not much on praying, but I'll do some tonight," she said. "Maybe all hell won't break loose."

"Maybe," he said, honesty holding back anything more. He returned to the ramshackle house with her, her lips demanding a last long kiss and then she padded silently to her room. He found a spare cot in another room, stretched out on it, and let sleep fill the few remaining hours till dawn, all too aware that time continued to tick away and the moment of savage retaliation grew closer.

6

Janice was up when he emerged from the house, a pale-green blouse and dark-green riding skirt, ash-blond hair silvery in the morning sun. She had just finished tightening the cinch on the bay when she saw him, stopped, and strode toward him, and he saw the copper fire in her eyes.

"Enjoy your reward last night?" she threw at him with waspish venom.

He let his brows lift in mind surprise. "Spying one of your pastimes, honey?" he asked.

"No spying. I happened to see you go off together and I waited. Curiosity, I guess," she snapped.

"You waited? Didn't get much sleep, then, did you?" He smiled.

Her eyes blazed back. "A young girl out here alone, grateful to you for saving her, and you had to take advantage of that," she accused.

"Held her at gunpoint," he said. "She liked the gun, too."

Janice's lips pressed hard on each other. "And now I suppose you're going to say that some women are more grateful than others," she flung at him.

"No," he said. "It's just that some women know what they want and some don't."

"I know perfectly well what I want," she hissed.

"Yes, you do," he agreed, and her blond brows

knitted together in surprise. "You just haven't listened to yourself yet."

"Bastard," she spit at him.

"Finish with your horse. We're leaving for Sam Rawley's place in a few minutes," he told her.

"Why do I have to go?" she asked.

"It'll help my story and a lot of lives might hang on his not getting suspicious," Fargo said.

"Is that the only reason?" she questioned, her eyes narrowing suspiciously. "Or don't you trust leaving me behind here?"

He smiled. "You can add that one on if you like," he said. "Now move your ass."

She spun, strode back to the bay, and he saw Tom Benton emerge from the house with Vicky. "Good luck," Benton said. "Keep your eyes open when you're there and you might see something worthwhile. But he's your man, believe me."

Vicky disappeared into the stable, returned on the horse that had pulled the runabout. Fargo climbed into the saddle and swung in beside her, glanced across at Janice. She met his eyes, moved the dark bay forward, swung in behind them, and stayed a half-dozen yards back as Vicky set out across the prairie. Vicky questioned him with her eyes, but he didn't respond. "You know Sam Rawley?" he asked instead.

"Met him a few times," she answered. "He's a hard man, Pa's right about that."

Fargo's face hardened. "Time's running out. Another bad raid and the tribes will explode."

"I'm sort of surprised they haven't by now," Vicky said, glanced back at Janice.

"There's a reason for that. This is hunting time, gathering hides, drying them, tanning them, doing the same with fur for robes. They're getting ready for winter. They're not anxious to take the warpath now, but they sure as hell will if the raids keep on," Fargo said.

Vicky nodded understanding, suddenly slowed her horse and waited as Janice came up. "Why are you staying back, Janice?" she asked.

"I prefer riding alone," Janice said, her blond coloring pale ice.

Vicky frowned. "What's got into you?" she asked.

Fargo laughed. "Nothing. That's the trouble," he said.

Janice's eyes blazed copper at him. "You're crude," she said. "Absolutely crude."

He met Vicky's frown. "Janice saw us come back last night," he said, and Vicky's eyes widened in instant understanding.

"I see," Vicky said, her eyes on Janice.

"I hardly think you do," Janice speared.

"Jealousy is bad for the system," Vicky said tartly.

"So are overactive glands," Janice snapped back, and Fargo watched Vicky's eyes darken in surprise and temper.

"Ride," he barked. "I've no time for cat fights." Vicky turned away, spurred her horse into a canter. He caught up to her after a moment to ride beside her. "Simmer down and slow down," he said. "You shot first. She shot back."

Vicky slowed her horse, let the set of her face relax. "Guess so," she admitted, settled down.

"Have second thoughts about last night?" he asked.

"No," she said quickly. "I'm only sorry the night wasn't longer."

They rode for another half-hour when he saw the buildings come into view, rising up on the flat prairie, and Vicki nodded at his glance. "Sam Rawley's spread," she said.

He motioned to Janice. "Get up here," he said. Her face stayed sullen as she brought the bay alongside him. "Look happy," Fargo said. "You're supposed to be going to marry me."

Her glance was acid. "I'm not that good an actress," she returned.

"Try," Fargo growled, his eyes watching Sam Rawley's spread take shape as he neared. Three large corrals came first—well-fenced, well-stocked with cattle—two freshly painted barns, and a main house, sturdy frame and log, with a bunkhouse in back. He saw a dozen cowhands at work, some in the corrals, others at fence-mending. He rode up to the main house, his eyes taking in the complete spread, lingering on the two riflemen standing guard at opposite sides of the corrals.

The man emerged from the house, fancy boots and a blue shirt, steel-gray hair and eyes to match in a blocky, square face with a harsh, tight mouth, a big man who almost glared with his every glance. His eyes stayed piercing, slowed, but didn't change as they came to Vicky. "Miss Benton," he said, his voice cold. "What brings you here?"

"These folks were looking for you. I brought them," Vicky said, gestured with one hand. "Skye Fargo and his fiancée, Miss Davidson."

Sam Rawley's steel-gray eyes turned to Fargo, waited.

"Heard you might have some good land and stock to sell," Fargo said with a nod.

"Sell?" Sam Rawley frowned. "I'm not selling anything. Hell, I want more land, not less."

"I heard you had enough and were looking to get rid of some," Fargo said blandly.

"You heard wrong, mister," Sam Rawley shot back.

Fargo paused, let his thoughts choose words. "I'd settle for some good stock," he said.

"No way. That's my breeding stock, brought all the way up from Texas, longhorn, mostly. I'm still seeing if they'll work out up here."

"Guess I wasted my time coming here," Fargo said.

"You did," Sam Rawley agreed brusquely.

"I heard the wrong things about you," Fargo said.

"It's easy to hear wrong things about me. I aim to be powerful, not popular," Sam Rawley said, his voice hard as the nails in the door behind him. "People can say or think whatever they like. Doesn't bother me any."

"The army thinks the Sioux and the others around here are taking the warpath," Fargo said.

"I'll take care of myself," Sam Rawley said.

"Heard somebody's stirring up the tribes," Fargo said.

"Maybe." The man shrugged. "Can't see a reason for doing that."

"Somebody has one," Fargo said as he backed the Ovaro a few paces. "We'll be going. Sorry we can't do business."

"Nobody around here's going to sell you land. Everybody wants it for themselves. They'll keep it 'less the Indians lift their scalps," Rawley said.

Fargo nodded, turned the horse and rode away, his eyes moving over Sam Rawley's spread again. The man could send out raiders in any direction, his place a central location facing the hills less than an hour away. And he seemed hard enough to do most anything he wanted. Yet it still didn't set right and Fargo swore inwardly. Vicky and Janice rode beside him and Vicky waited till they'd cleared the Rawley place before she commented. "I think

Pa's right. Rawley's hard, land-hungry, ruthless. You heard him yourself, he doesn't care what anyone says or thinks about him. He's behind it, I'm convinced now," she said.

"Maybe," Fargo grunted.

"Just maybe?" Vicky questioned, and he caught a glance of curiosity Janice gave him.

He considered saying more, decided against it. "Maybe," he repeated.

"He's so gracious about explanations," Janice said tartly.

Fargo didn't answer, rode in silence till they returned to Vicky's place. Hank Thorst was there, Fargo noted at once, as he saw the horse outside. But only Tom Benton emerged as they rode up, questions in his eyes. "Find anything that'll help you?" Tom Benton asked.

"No," Fargo said.

"You see enough to decide he's your man?" Tom Benton questioned.

"He could be," Fargo said.

"Fargo's not convinced," Vicky said, and he heard the touch of annoyance in her tone. He saw Tom Benton frown in thought for a moment.

"Hank stopped by to talk business, but he told me something he heard up in Prairie Dog," the man said.

"Dolly Westin's town. You know Dolly?" Fargo asked.

"Who doesn't? Only gal mayor in any of the territories. Can't say I know her personally, though," Tom Benton said. "I take it you do."

"We're old friends," Fargo said. "What'd your man hear?"

"Two men talking about meeting others on Rollaway Ridge tomorrow just before sundown," Tom

Benton said. "Now, the Crow usually make hunting camp back of Rollaway Ridge. Could be they've one there now."

"And that could be the next raid planned," Fargo said. "Where's Rollaway Ridge?"

"First hill north, behind Three Altar Rocks," the man said.

"I'll be there come dusk tomorrow," Fargo said.

"I'd go with you," Vicky's father began, "but with these coughing spells I could blow everything if they came at the wrong time."

"Could and would," Fargo agreed. "I like working alone, anyway."

Tom Benton nodded. "Now, you'll excuse me. Got a lot of things to go over with Hank before he leaves," he said.

"Got enough stew left for a good meal," Vicky said.

"Enjoy it. I'll be riding out now," Fargo said. "There's still good light left."

"When will you be back?" she asked.

"After dark sometime. They don't raid the camps by night. They want to be able to see what they're up against," Fargo told her.

"Be careful," Vicky said as she took her horse into the barn.

"You leaving me here alone?" he heard Janice ask waspishly. "Aren't you afraid I'll skip out?"

"No," he said.

Her blond brows arched. "Sudden trust? I'm touched."

"Don't be. Trust hasn't a thing to do with it," he said. "I just think you've seen enough now to know that you'd wind up under some big buck if you tried running on your own."

Her silence was its own answer, and he watched

her dismount and go into the house. He turned the Ovaro and rode, headed north into the low hills. At the first one he scanned the terrain, moved up the slope slowly until he found the three huge rocks, flat, piled half atop each other as though they were altarpieces. He rode past the rocks and found Rollaway Ridge, one side falling off sharply to give it its name. Beyond the ridge, he saw the stand of forest and moved the Ovaro toward it as his eyes scoured the ground. Indian pony tracks were plentiful and he found a line of them into the trees, dismounted, trailed on foot. The tracks led single-file, a straight line, and Fargo halted, his glance noting the light that faded fast.

He turned back. He had seen enough to satisfy himself that there was an Indian camp not too far away. He returned to Rollaway Ridge in the last of the light, rode just beneath the crest, sought a place that suited him. He finally found it, marked it in his mind, and headed back toward Vicky's as night descended. He rode slowly, let thoughts turn inside him. If Tom Benton's information proved right, he might be able to buy a little more of that precious time he needed and once more stay the bloody shadow of savage massacre.

But that's all it would be, another stay, a reprieve, unless he could nail down who was behind the raids. His thoughts went to Sam Rawley, and once again he couldn't accept the man's guilt—not yet, at least. Questions still nagged at him, things that refused to fit right. Rawley would remain a question mark a little longer.

Fargo saw the dark bulk of Vicky's house come into view under the moonlight. He had just neared the small cluster of black locust trees when the figure stepped into view, slender, dark-brown hair, looking tall in a gray nightdress that reached the grass. He halted, slid to the ground.

"Couldn't sleep," Vicky said solemnly. "Came out here to wait for you."

"Worrying or wanting?" Fargo grinned.

"Both," she said as she led the way into the trees. At the place where they had been the night before she halted, turned to him, dropped to her knees, reached out, and pulled him down beside her. "I don't know how many nights are left for us, for anybody. I don't want to waste even one," she said.

"Not much for waste, myself," Fargo agreed.

She pulled a string at the neck of the nightdress and it came open. A wriggle of her shoulders brought the top tumbling down, and she sat before him on her knees, upturned little breasts beautifully imploring, a naked penitent before the altar of desire. She helped him shed clothes, fell onto him as he pulled pants away, legs drawn up, seeking him at once. She found his throbbing, aroused maleness and enveloped him in her warm, wet tunnel, moving her hips up and down instantly, her breath a short gasp of satisfaction.

"God, oh, God, Fargo," Vicky murmured. "It's all I've thought about since last night."

He turned with her, rolled atop her, pressed his mouth over her breasts, sucked one and then the other, and she cried out, pushed her hips upward, and he moved quickly inside her, short, almost-rough thrustings. "Yes, yes, yes ... Jesus, yes," Vicky Benton screamed, and she matched his every move with her own push. She came quickly and he let himself come with her, exploding with her warm contractions. She screamed, a half-sobbing scream, and she fell back, her body pulsing, slender legs twitching against him. He heard her words, whispered sounds, her eyes closed. "So much, so little," she breathed.

He drew from her and she uttered a tiny cry of protest, half-turned, and pressed herself against him, little firm nipples pushing into his chest. She seemed to sleep, but he knew she was only gathering herself and he smiled when her hand crept along his leg, seeking, finding. She caressed gently for a few moments, but he felt her begin to grow tense, her mouth seeking him, the wanting take command of her. He turned for her and once again, the still prairie night echoed to her ecstasies until finally she lay beside him, surfeited. As the night began to wind itself down, she stirred finally, sat up, and slipped into the nightdress.

"What happens if you don't come back tomorrow, Fargo?" she asked as she watched him pull on clothes.

"I figure to be back," he told her.

"What happens if you don't?" she insisted.

"I suggest you and your pa leave, run for it, don't wait any longer," he answered.

"Pa's got things packed for that, just in case," she said. "But he'll stay on to the last moment." Fargo shrugged and she peered at him. "What happens to Janice?"

"Take her with you," he said.

Vicky's arms reached around his neck. "Don't go tomorrow. Maybe it's too late to stop it," she said.

"There's a chance yet," he said. "Can't turn away from it now."

She nodded unhappily, walked back to the house in silence with him, paused at the doorway. "I wanted so to run, to get away from here," she said.

"Now I want to stay, wait for you, be with you. Now it's all different."

"Nothing's different," he told her, his voice suddenly harsh.

She peered at him, studied his face, and slowly turned and disappeared into the house.

Fargo drew a deep sigh, followed her in, and stretched out on the extra cot. Desire was a two-faced mistress: a wonderful, warm, exciting one and a mocking distorter of reality. But then he'd learned that long ago, other arms and other places. He closed his eyes, let sleep come till the new day.

7

The big man with the lake-blue eyes sat silent as a stone at the place he'd marked for himself just below Rollaway Ridge. The day drifted slowly to dusk and he'd tucked the Ovaro out of sight behind two tall rocks, sat with the big Sharps rifle in his lap. Vicky had stayed silent, almost morose for most of the day, and he'd seen her snap at her father twice. But Janice had echoed her question as he'd saddled the Ovaro and prepared to leave.

"What happens if you don't get back?" she'd asked.

"Worried about me?" he'd laughed. "Or about yourself?"

"Maybe some of both," she'd said, and he'd laughed again. "What's so funny?" she'd questioned sharply.

"Nothing, really. Just echoes. Run with the Bentons if I don't get back," he'd told her.

"I think I'd rather run by myself," she'd said, and she'd seen the expression in his eyes. "No, not because of her. It's him."

"Vicky's pa?" Fargo had frowned.

Janice had shrugged. "He bothers me. He's nice and pleasant, but those eyes . . . they're so strange. They never stop burning. Something about that man frightens me. I can't explain it. I just feel it."

Fargo had studied her, no sullenness in her delicate blond loveliness now, only a frowning somberness. Her words had circled inside him and he'd found himself unable to dismiss them.

"Let me go with you," she'd said.

He had shaken his head. "I'll be back," he'd told her, and he'd watched her eyes stay on him, accept without accepting. She'd turned from him, stayed in the house, but he'd seen her ash-blond hair at the window, watching as he'd ridden off.

He broke off thoughts as he caught movement on the ridge, slid down farther along the ground, and saw the two riders appear. Behind them, the gray violet of dusk was starting to tint the horizon. The two men sat their horses, plainly waiting, and a few minutes later two more riders appeared, coming up along the near side of the ridge. Three more joined them, coming up the hill in a gallop, slowing to a halt as they reached the others. As he watched, the riders started down the other side of the ridge, headed for the trees.

Fargo half-rose, rested his elbow on one knee, and raised the Sharps. He'd picked the spot because it gave cover and let him see both sides of Rollaway Ridge. Seven riders, he grunted, but that proved little of itself. They could have met for other reasons, and he waited, watched. They continued on toward the trees and he saw the first one slow, point to the pony tracks on the ground. Fargo's mouth tightened. He'd seen enough. He sighted along the long barrel of the big Sharps, fired, and the rider bringing up the rear toppled from his horse. The others spun their horses, and Fargo aimed again, fired two quick shots. The first sent one more rider falling from his horse; the second missed, and he saw the others break up, race off in different directions. He followed with the rifle a rider racing toward the trees, fired again, and the man pitched forward over the neck of his horse, fell as a low branch clutched at him as he went by.

The others had taken cover, three over the crest of the ridge, two behind the rock formations. Fargo moved back, listened for the sound of horses in flight. But there was only silence. They had decided not to flee, and he swore softly, their actions unexpected. The edge of the rock beside him suddenly exploded in a shower of chips as the shot echoed; he threw himself flat, looked up to see two of the men atop the ridge on their stomachs. They crawled back, spotted him, and a second volley of shots exploded, too close.

Fargo moved back toward where he'd hidden the Ovaro, stayed behind the few rocks that afforded protection. Hoofbeats resounded suddenly and he glimpsed two riders race up and over the far end of the ridge, out of rifle range but making a long circle to come up behind him.

He swore again. That left a fifth man who was probably circling to his right. The dusk had drifted in, shooting light growing precarious. He moved back, slipped around the rock to the Ovaro, and drew a pair of quick shots as he stepped into the open for a moment. He pulled himself onto the horse, reloaded the Sharps, and stuck it into the saddle holster. He drew his Colt and flattened himself against the pinto, waited a moment longer, and sent the horse racing from behind the rocks at a gallop. Three shots exploded, all wide of their mark, and he raced toward the line of trees, saw the two on horseback racing toward him. He held fire, distance and dusk combining to make accurate shooting almost impossible. He reached the trees, went into the timber a few feet, and reined up to leap from the saddle, drop down at the edge of the treeline.

The two on horseback neared and he scanned the ridge beyond, saw the other two there had retrieved their horses and headed down. The fifth man appeared, to his right, converging at a gallop. Fargo waited until the nearest two came within range. He fired, saw the one rider lose his hat, duck, and whirl his horse away. He fired again, two fast shots— for effect more than accuracy—and the other rider wheeled away.

Fargo rose, staying in the trees, ran a dozen yards to his left in his long-strided lope. The horsemen merged into two groups, avoided the spot where he had been, and started toward the trees. There was little light left as he fired; the attackers wheeled away in surprise, halted out of range.

Fargo retraced steps inside the treeline, went another dozen yards in the other direction. The five horsemen started toward him again, shifting their path almost directly in front of him. He fired and saw them rein up in alarm and surprise. They had seen only one man, but he knew what they wondered now: perhaps there were others. He saw them draw back, fade from sight in the new darkness, and he listened to the sounds of their horses moving up the slope to the ridge. He could barely glimpse the dark shapes for an instant as they crested the top of the ridge and disappeared down the other side.

He rose, holstered the Colt with grim satisfaction. The raid was turned away. Any Indian encampment would have heard the shots and be up and on guard; the raiders knew that as well as he did.

He retrieved the Ovaro and moved from the trees,

rode slowly up the slope to the ridge. The moon was too low yet to afford anything but a glimmer of light, and he reached the top of the ridge, paused, started to move forward when the volley of shots split the darkness. He felt one bullet graze his temple, another his shoulder as he dropped low in the saddle, kicked the Ovaro into a gallop. The horse leaped forward and Fargo found another reason for the ridge's name as the pinto lost its footing, half-fell, half-slid sideways. Rollaway Ridge not only fell off sharply at one side, but the ground was soft and loose and rolled away under a horse. He felt himself falling from the saddle, hit the ground, rolled downward as more shots exploded, none close now. He seized hold of a piece of brush, halted his roll, pulled himself up. Bastards, he swore softly. They'd lain in wait for him, determined to retrieve something out of the night.

He lay unmoving in the darkness and his ears picked up the sounds below, murmured voices, saddle leather creaking. They were mounting, moving off, and he felt the burning on his temple, shook his head, felt his vision fogging. He listened, heard the horses riding away. They were satisfied they'd gotten him. Feeling his eyes clouding again, he lay still, waited till the hoofbeats faded away. He started to get up, used the bush as a handle, reached his feet, and felt the dizziness sweep over him. He managed to grab the bush as he fell, his hand closing around it, slipping away as he rolled down the slope to lay at the bottom in a half-world, neither conscious nor unconscious.

The strange, twilight world stayed on him, a place where he lay still, dimly aware of sounds, scents, seeing only through a gray curtain. He had no idea how long he'd lain in the half-world when slowly the gray curtain began to lift itself from his eyes. He stared upward at stars, a black sky, and sounds came to him no longer wrapped in distance. He was on his back, he realized. He pushed himself up on both elbows and his temple hurt. He rose to his feet, waited for the dizziness to sweep around him, but he was steady. He drew in a deep breath and flexed muscles. The moon had trailed halfway across the sky, he saw, realized he had lain semiconscious for hours. He glanced around in the darkness, whistled, and saw the white of the Ovaro's mid-section gleaming through the night, moving toward him. The horse came up to him and halted, whinnied, and Fargo leaned his face into the powerful neck, held there for a moment, and then pulled himself into the saddle. He felt the scrape along his temple as he rode, ran one finger over the narrow line, and realized how close death had passed by.

He headed the Ovaro through the last of the night and finally reached Vicky's house, silent and dark. He unsaddled the Ovaro and went inside, found the cot, had his shirt off when he saw the figure in the doorway, ash-blond hair unmistakable even in the darkness. He saw Vicky appear, seconds after, smaller, slenderer, standing a half-step behind Janice. Both stared at him, waited.

"They came," he said wearily. "I turned them away. Got three of them." He lay down on the cot, stretched.

"Want anything?" Vicky asked.

"Sleep" he said; he closed his eyes and let weariness sweep him into almost-instant slumber. Dimly he heard the two figures move from the room.

When morning came, he woke to find a large basin of cold water and a washcloth beside the cot. He rose, washed, smelled coffee, and hurried dressing. In the front room, he found Tom Benton with Vicky and Janice, the coffepot over a low flame in the fireplace. The man's intense blue eyes focused on him as he entered.

"Heard you did it," Tom Benton said. "Got three of them, Vicky told me."

Fargo nodded and took a tin cup of coffee from Vicky, drank deeply of it at once.

"I figure you ought to pay Sam Rawley a visit, see if he's real upset."

"Soon as I finish this coffee," Fargo agreed. "If it was his crew, and he lost three of them, I ought to be able to pick up some signs." He saw Vicky turn to him, her lips start to part. "I'll be going alone," he said flatly. "I could run into trouble."

Her eyes accepted his remark and he drained the coffee, went outside to saddle the Ovaro.

Tom Benton came out to him as he was just tightening the cinch. "You watch Rawley. He's tricky," the man said. "He'll have some sort of story ready if you get him into a corner. But you're on the right trail and don't you forget it."

Fargo nodded, swung onto the pinto, and rode away at a steady trot; he kept the pace up as Tom Benton's words stayed with him. The man was convinced of Sam Rawley's guilt and his conviction was deep. Maybe right, also, Fargo mused. But the maybe still clung, and he quickened the horse's pace until he came into sight of Sam Rawley's spread. He rode past the corrals, saw most of the men gathered in front of the bunkhouse, steered the horse toward them. He saw Sam Rawley amid the men, hatless, his steel-gray hair easy to spot.

As Fargo rode up, he saw the big Owensboro Huckster wagon pulled up in front of the bunkhouse, with the drop endgate open. He came to a halt as six cowhands carried a pine coffin from the bunk-house and slid it onto the wagon. Fargo saw Sam Rawley's hard eyes come to rest on him. "You back, mister?" the man growled.

"Passing by," Fargo said, his eyes on the pine box. "One of your men?" he asked.

Sam Rawley's face was harsh as he nodded, and Fargo watched the six hands carry another pine box to the wagon. A third followed, slid onto the wagon, and the endgate was pulled up and closed. Fargo's eyes stayed on Sam Rawley, questioned, and the man bit out words. "Lost three men," he said. "Three good men."

"Accident?" Fargo asked softly.

"No accident," the man snapped. "They were shot, gunned down last night."

"Where?" Fargo probed.

"Right here," Rawley said. "A torch went through the bunkhouse window. Everybody ran outside and three of them were gunned down, shots fired from out in the darkness. They were gone before my boys could get themselves together, whoever they were."

"They?" Fargo echoed.

"Had to be more than one, the way the shots came, picked off my three men instantly, then hightailed it," Rawley said. "Can't figure it at all."

"There was a try at raiding one of the Indian camps last night," Fargo said, his eyes riveted on Sam Rawley. "Three of the raiders were killed."

The man's eyes grew harder. "You saying something, Fargo?" he rasped.

Fargo's chiseled face remained expressionless. "Not yet. Kind of a funny coincidence, though, isn't it?" he said.

Sam Rawley took a step closer to the big man on

the Ovaro and his face grew red. "That's just what it is, a goddamn coincidence," he roared. "I told you what happened to my three men. You calling me a liar, mister?"

"Not calling anybody anything," Fargo said quietly. "Not yet." He pulled the Ovaro around, slowly rode away, and felt Sam Rawley's eyes boring into his back. He rode on, letting the horse walk as thoughts turned inside him. Coincidence? he grunted. Or a hastily concocted story? Coincidence has a long arm, but is it this long? he mused. But he had no choice now. He'd have to watch Sam Rawley's place. It would tie him down, and if Rawley were behind the raids, he could be drawing the raiders from someplace else. But he'd have to take that risk. Sam Rawley seemed to be fulfilling Tom Benton's and Major Keyser's convictions.

Vicky came out to meet him when he reached the ramshackle house, Janice following on her heels and Tom Benton emerging a moment later, his intense eyes peering anxiously.

Fargo dismounted, his sentences terse as he told of what he'd found and of Sam Rawley's answers.

"He must take you for a fool with that kind of story," Vicky's father said. "But then he had to come up with a story on short notice."

Fargo nodded, glanced at Vicky as she looked at him. "Pa was right all along," she said, and he heard the surge of pride in her voice.

"I told you I was," her father said gleefully, his eyes going to the big man with the chiseled face. "He had to go fetch the three you brought down. He couldn't risk one being alive and talking," Tom Benton said.

Fargo nodded again, the man's words entirely

logical. "I'll be setting up watch at Rawley's place," he said.

"When?" Vicky asked.

"Right now," Fargo answered. "Just came back to tell you what I saw and to get some fresh water in my canteen."

"I've some jerky you can take with you," Vicky said. She turned, hurried into the house, and her father followed.

Fargo met Janice's hazel eyes as she came to him, her voice low, her gaze quietly appraising. "You're not convinced about Sam Rawley," she said. "You can't afford not to watch him, but you're still holding back on him."

"What makes you say that?" he asked as he silently raged at the accuracy of female instinct.

"I just know. Tell me I'm wrong," she challenged.

"I'm not telling you anything," he said, and knew the reply was weak.

"Take me with you," Janice said, her voice dropping to a whisper. "I told you I can't stand that man."

"No way. You stay put," he answered.

"How long will you watch?" she asked.

He shrugged. "Can't say. Maybe only a day, maybe a week."

"I won't stay a week here alone," Janice said.

"Don't be a fool. You stay here till I get back," he ordered.

She went into the house, no sullenness in her any longer, but he saw her draw her lips in with a grimness that made him almost feel sorry for her. He was on the Ovaro when Vicky came out with the package of jerky.

"Be careful, Fargo," she murmured, and her eyes held hope and promise. She reached up, held his hand for a moment, and stepped back, hurried into the house as he rode off.

He held a fast trot as he made his way back, slowed only when he began to draw near Sam Rawley's place. The prairie was a flat table in every direction and he grimaced, moved forward slowly, and found a collection of shad scale, their scruffy foliage just enough to hide the Ovaro. Barely within sight of Rawley's spread, he dismounted, settled down, aware that the flat land was a help as well as a hindrance. He'd easily spot any riders leaving the ranch for the hills. Even in the moonlight they'd stand out against the flat land. He made himself comfortable and watched the dusk turn the prairie into soft violet. The dark came, the moon lifted itself into the sky, and his eyes stayed on the distant buildings. The low bellow of cattle drifted across the silence but nothing moved from the ranch, not even a lone rider.

He watched till the night was deep and then let himself sleep, woke with the new day's light. He could see the ranch come to life, distant shapes tiny as toy figures. The day seemed endless, interrupted only by the arrival of two riders bringing in a handful of young calves. Night finally came again and Fargo strained his eyes as he scanned the ranch, and once again no riders moved from the place. He felt the uneasiness stabbing at him, but he stayed, let another morning break and the day grow long.

The uneasiness became apprehension. Something was wrong. He felt it inside himself. If Rawley were behind the raids, he wasn't sending out his raiders from the ranch. Fargo swore silently. He'd wasted three days and nights in fruitless watching while all hell could be about to break loose. If the raiders hadn't struck again, they'd have to strike soon. The kettle had to be kept boiling until it overflowed.

But he stayed through the day, eyes on Sam Rawley's place, let another dusk come, another night follow, and he saw no riders leave the ranch. He slept when the dawn drew near, woke with the morning, and watched for a few hours more until, his lips pulled tight, he took the Ovaro and stole away from his hiding place, backed the pinto carefully out of the shad scale, and rode back across the flat land to the Benton place. Vicky was first to see him near, rushed from the house as he swung down from the saddle to lean into his chest, arms clasped around him.

"I was getting real worried. I wanted to go look for you, but Pa said not to," she murmured.

"He was right," Fargo said as she pulled back and he saw Tom Benton step from the house, intense eyes searching his face.

"Seen enough?" the man asked excitedly.

"Didn't see anything. Nobody rode from his place," Fargo said, unable to keep the annoyance from his voice. "If he's behind it, he's working it from somewhere else."

"He's behind it. You'll just have to watch him some more. I'd guess he's probably laying low for a spell," Benton said.

"He can't afford that, not if he wants to push the tribes onto the warpath. Isolated raids won't do it," Fargo said. "They're ready to explode. They just need one more push. This wouldn't be the time to pull back and lay low."

"What do you figure to do?" the man asked.

"Ride, hunt, scout, maybe get lucky. I've lost four days sitting outside Sam Rawley's spread.

Maybe I'm four days too late now. I've got to find out," Fargo said angrily.

"Making a mistake, Fargo. Hang in at Rawley's place. You'll get your lead there," Tom Benton said.

"Where's Janice?" Fargo asked, saw the quick glance exchanged between Vicky and her father.

"She took off," Vicky said. "She'd been getting edgier and edgier. We couldn't stop her."

"Wasn't my business to do so," Tom Benton said. "She's big enough to know what she's doing."

"When?" Fargo barked.

"Just a few hours ago," Vicki said. "She said she was going to try to make Fort Kearny."

"Goddamn," Fargo swore. "She won't have a snowball in hell's chance." He whirled the pinto, rode a few dozen yards north, and saw the bay's hoofprints leading away from the house.

"Forget her. Stay with Rawley," Tom Benton called.

"I'll be back when and if," Fargo said, and spurred the pinto into a gallop.

Janice's tracks were fresh and easy to follow. She had taken a straight line northwest, over the low hills, bordered the timber stands. He rode hard and the Ovaro's ground-eating stride made good time. He saw that she had halted frequently, walked the bay slowly, cautiously. She was picking her way, trying to be careful, he grunted. The Ovaro continued to devour distance and the day had begun to slide toward dusk when he spotted her, spurred the pinto forward. She heard him, looked back, and halted. Her eyes were wide with relief when he reined up beside her.

"You are one damn-fool girl," he roared.

"I'm sorry," she said, the answer unexpected,

disarming, defusing his anger. Her hazel eyes stayed round. "God, I'm glad to see you," Janice said.

"This is something new," Fargo commented.

"I thought something had gone wrong, that maybe you wouldn't be coming back," she said, and he saw only honesty in her eyes. "I stayed as long as I could. I just couldn't stay there with him any longer. Those eyes were driving me up a wall, and then that business partner of his, Hank Thorst, came back yesterday. He's almost as bad as Tom Benton. He never smiles and he hardly took his eyes off me. I wasn't going to wait for him to come back again, not with you maybe never coming back."

Fargo drew a deep sigh. "No matter, you should've stayed," he said.

"I would've if I'd thought you were coming back," Janice said, her hazel eyes growing almost apologetic. "Thanks for coming after me," she murmured. "What'd you find out at Sam Rawley's?"

"Nothing, dammit," he bit out angrily. "Wasted four days, maybe blew it altogether, and I still don't have a handle on it."

"And you still don't buy Sam Rawley," Janice said, eyes narrowing at him. "Everything points to him and you still hold back. Why?"

Fargo looked past her, made no reply.

"I think I've a right to know. You dragged me in on this thing. I ought to at least know what you're thinking, Fargo."

He met her eyes, turned her words in his mind. "Maybe you do have a right knowing that," he agreed. "There's more than one thing sticks in me about Sam Rawley. First, whoever's behind this knows the Indians damn well, knows their hunting patterns, where they make their travel camps, their habits. I don't see Rawley knowing that."

"Maybe he's had his men out scouting, finding out those things," Janice offered.

"Possible, but it takes years to learn those things," Fargo said.

"What else?" Janice asked.

"It doesn't make any damn sense for Rawley to want an uprising. As a plan for using the Indians to get rid of the settlers it doesn't make any damn sense. He'd be bringing it all down on his head, and he put a lot of work into that spread. The Indians aren't going to pick and choose."

"Benton thinks Rawley's convinced he has enough men to stand them off," Janice said.

"He'd need three times that many," Fargo said. "He's a hard man, but he's no fool."

"People miscalculate. They make mistakes, don't think things through enough," she answered.

He turned her words over. "Possible," he agreed.

"There's something more," Janice prodded.

"One thing, and it sticks hardest in me." She waited as he chose words. "Rawley's land hungry, but if he's behind it, it isn't just a clever way to get land. This means wholesale slaughter, massacre, hell breaking loose here and now. There's hate behind this, not greed. There's rage, sickness, not ruthlessness. It doesn't fit Sam Rawley."

"Unless he's sick. Maybe you're missing that," she said.

"Maybe," Fargo conceded. "Let's move."

"Where?" Janice asked.

"Prairie Dog. Might pick up something there," he said.

"And you'll see Dolly Westin," Janice bristled. "You were on your way to see her in the first place."

He grinned, nodded.

"Combining things again?" she speared tartly.

"Why not?" he answered.

"Damn, Fargo, is that all you think about, sleeping with every woman?" Janice accused.

He let himself look hurt. "Dolly's the mayor. Would I be going there to sleep with a mayor?" he asked.

"You'd sleep with a preacher if he were a woman," she threw back.

He let his lips purse. "Not a bad idea. You could get balled and blessed at the same time," he said.

Her lips were thinned in anger, her eyes sending out copper sparks. "What am I supposed to do while you're off . . . off . . ." she stammered, searched for words.

"Seeing Dolly?" he finished.

"Screwing the mayor," she exploded.

"You have a dirty mind, Janice," he chided.

"Hah!" she snorted.

"There's a hotel in Prairie Dog. I'll get you a nice room for the night," he said.

She threw him an acid glance and made no reply as he headed down the hillside, found a path that became a road.

The night slipped over the land before they reached Prairie Dog, but he saw wagon tracks on the road, followed them, and the buildings of the town finally came into view, dark shapes in the night. Janice brought her bay up close to him as they rode down the main street, mostly dark, but the light and sound in the center of town located the saloon.

Fargo halted, found that the only hotel was built over the saloon, with a separate side-by-side entrance. Two saloon girls in tight dresses lounged in the doorway of the saloon. He dropped the Ovaro's reins over the hitching post, waited as Janice dismounted, and followed her into the hotel entrance.

A window at the right looked into the saloon and the off-pitch tinkle of a player piano carried into the hotel lobby. A man wearing shirtsleeves and a stained vest peered from behind the front desk.

"Room for the young lady," Fargo said, and glanced at Janice. She stared through the window into the saloon where a girl in a gold-beaded short dress danced with a huge bearded man and two other girls sat on customers' laps. Still another saloon girl did a poor shimmy in one corner to the applause of an uncritical audience.

"Sign here," the desk clerk said, and Janice took her eyes from the window to sign the register with swift, angry strokes. "First room next floor," the man said.

Fargo took the key and led Janice up the short flight of steps, opened the door and turned the lamp on. A brass bed, battered dresser, and one chair filled the small room, and he saw the distaste in Janice's face. "You'll get a good night's sleep," he said.

She leveled a cool stare at him. "I might just go down to the saloon. It looked like they were having fun there," she said.

"Is that so?" he said.

Her eyes spit fire. "I'm not going to sit here and twiddle my thumbs while you're twiddling the mayor," she flung at him.

"There you go again, jumping to conclusions," Fargo said.

"Then see your friend and be back in an hour," she challenged.

"Got too much to talk about." He grinned. "And your jealousy's showing again."

"It's not jealousy. It's respect for proper behavior," she snapped.

"You offering anything for me to come back early?" He laughed.

"Come back early and see," she returned quickly.

"Give you another chance," he said. "You know, a bird in hand."

"Go to hell," she hissed as he closed the door. She was made of contradictions, he pondered, all of a turmoil inside. He hurried down the steps, paused at the desk. "Where do I find Dolly Westin?" he asked.

"Reckon she'd be to home by now," the man said. "Small white house with green shutters, other end of town."

Fargo stepped into the night and rode the Ovaro slowly down the street. Prairie Dog had a church, he noted. A bank, too. The rest of it was pretty much the same as most prairie towns, filled with men on their way someplace else and women willing to go with them. In the case of Prairie Dog, they moved into the Montana Territory or took the trail west to the Rockies. Few went much farther than that, the great mountain range a barrier to all but the most determined or the most desperate.

He slowed as he reached the end of town and espied the little house with the green shutters; he moved the horse in front and dismounted. A lamp burned in one of the windows and he knocked on the door, his glance noting the small sign that read MAYOR DOLLY WESTIN—RESIDENCE.

"Classy," he murmured aloud as the door opened and Dolly stared out at him. He saw the surprise gather in her face, took in the blond hair, still out of a bottle, her broad face still pretty enough with deep-blue eyes that were quick to laugh, a wide, full mouth made for all kinds of sensual pleasures. The rest of Dolly Westin was as he'd remembered her, overflowing, almost huge breasts not at all dismayed by the robe she wore, ample hips, and he was certain, the same surprisingly slender legs.

Dolly's full, red lips stayed open for a moment longer, finally formed words, her voice husky as always. "God damn," she breathed. "God damn." Her arms leaped upward, closed around him, pulled him into the room as she pressed the door shut. "Fargo," Dolly said. "Hot damn." Her breasts, pillowy and downy-soft, pressed against him as she hugged him to her. "You did get my letter," she said. "I'd begun to think it never reached you."

"It's in my pocket," he said. He pressed his lips on hers, and her soft, wide mouth opened at once, drew him in, full, soft lips, but then everything about Dolly was full and soft.

"God, it's good to see you, Fargo, except it brings back too many memories," Dolly said, her arm around him as she walked him into the house, neatly furnished, good solid wooden pieces, a gold settee at one side of the room, a polished oak bureau, even a painting of an eagle in flight on one wall.

"It's going well, isn't it?" he said.

"Real well. As mayor, I get a little piece of all the action in town. Nothing big, but plenty for me," Dolly answered. She swung around to face him. "I've waited so long for you to come this way. You're no good for a woman. You're the kind she can't forget," Dolly said.

"Nobody else?" he asked.

"Nobody, and they wouldn't be you, anyway. Being

126

a mayor cramps your style," she said. "You've got to be that big word for sneaky."

"Circumspect," he said.

"That's it." Dolly laughed. "And there's nobody worth being circumspect for. Until now." She undid the belt that held her robe at the waist and the garment fell open. Her big breasts ballooned out at once, very round, very soft, large brownish areolas, and he smiled in remembering, tiny nipples that were almost lost on the abundant breasts.

She drew him into the bedroom, done in pink, pulled off pink bloomers, and threw the robe from her as she fell back onto the bed. The high, very rounded pubic mound and the thick black nap caught his eye at once. It had always been especially sensuous with Dolly, fleshed, high, rounded little dome and its tangly black cap, symbolizing the earthy, encompassing sexuality that was her very being. It aroused him at once, memory and desire, yesterday and today all mingling together. He buried his face into the soft, big, pillowy breasts, bit down on each, not particularly gently, and he heard Dolly's eager laughter. He circled the brownish areola with his teeth, nibbling his way around the mark, and Dolly's arms came up, hands pulling at his shoulders.

Her legs drew apart, the rounded little pubic mound lifting, pushing upward, and she made raspy noises in her throat. "Come on, come on, Fargo," she gasped out as he let his hands push down across her breasts, down past her rib cage, pause on her rounded belly, and then press down hard on the fleshy mound, pushing fingers through the tangly black cap. "Oh, Jesus," Dolly cried out. "Fargo . . . Fargo."

He saw her heels dig into the bed as she pushed her full-fleshed pelvis upward, and he came over her, his organ eager, pulsing. He slid into Dolly and she gave a half-scream of pleasure, pulled him to her with her hands clasped around his back. He drew back, rammed forward, harshly, roughly, rammed forward again.

"Jesus, yes . . . you remember . . . yes, more, more," Dolly cried out.

He moved forward again, once again, began the rhythm of his rough, hard, ramrod thrusts. Dolly pushed her torso upward, met his every harsh motion. "More . . . more, harder, harder, oh, Christ, harder," she screamed. She was big inside and few men could fill her, satisfy her, she'd told him once, but he infused her, pressed, flesh rubbing flesh, and he rode her harshly, almost savagely, and she screamed for more, laughed, half-cried; and it was the way it had always been with Dolly: raw, unsubtle, physical sex, a primitive surge that fed on itself, engulfed, immersed, approached the edge of brutality.

"Yes, oh, Jesus . . . more, more, more," Dolly screamed, and the big breasts rolled against his face and he bit their softly smothering smoothness, somehow found one of the tiny nipples, and pulled on it. He felt Dolly suddenly quiver, her belly pushing up against him, and her legs drew up, knees digging into his ribs. "Jesus . . . aaaaaah . . . aaaaaooooooiiiiiiii . . ." she screamed. "I'm coming, I'm coming. More, harder, harder."

Fargo saw her arms fling out, backward, hands dig into the bedsheets, and the big breasts shook as the scream spiraled, grew, seemed to fill the room. For Dolly, the climax was not simply coming, not just an orgasm, but an upheaval, a turning inside out, an eruption of ecstasy that carried him with her. When he finally stopping his thrusting, he lay atop her, felt his own breath returning.

"Oh, Jesus, Fargo," Dolly breathed, her hands around him as he rested his face against the pillowed mounds. "You've got to stay awhile."

He rolled from her, lay beside her, and one breast rested against his cheek. "Can't, not this time," he said, and Dolly turned on her side to peer at him, a little frown furrowing her brow. "Damn, that's not fair," she protested.

"I'll come back," he said. "If I'm still in one piece. You heard about Indian trouble?"

Dolly nodded. "Heard talk of the Sioux and some of the others taking the warpath."

"It's hanging close," Fargo said.

Dolly's face grew somber. "Guess we'd be safe enough here in town. They'd most likely sweep south and west. God, all those settlers scattered through the territory, they'll be slaughtered."

"Somebody wants them to take the warpath," Fargo said grimly. "I've been trying to head it off."

"My God, who'd want that to happen?" Dolly frowned.

"You know Sam Rawley?" he asked, and she nodded. "Some folks have said he's behind it."

Dolly stared back as her thoughts raced, the frown deepening on her forehead. "Rawley's a hard man, greedy, usually gets what he wants," she said, "but this takes a monster." She paused, shrugged. "Maybe he is," she finished.

"I need something, anything to help me head it off. You hear anything that'd help?" Fargo asked.

Dolly thought for a moment, shook her head. "Lots of people pass through town. A lot talk at the saloon when the liquor loosens them up. They don't come confiding in me," she said. "I can ask for you."

"Time's damn near gone, Dolly," Fargo said. "And Sam Rawley's the only lead so far. Tom Benton's convinced he's the one."

"Who?" Dolly asked.

"Tom Benton," Fargo said. "He's got a broken-down place south of Rollaway Ridge. Lives there with his daughter."

"Thin man, funny blue eyes that look through you," she said, and Fargo nodded. "So he's come back," Dolly murmured.

Fargo felt his brows knit. "Come back?"

"Tom Benton used to be Indian agent for this half of the territory, was here for years," Dolly said.

Fargo felt the frown dig deeper, a stab of uneasiness push at him. "Used to be?" he questioned.

"He was caught running bad beef, stealing government funds, making deals with the Indians, whiskey in exchange for top pelts and hides. He even did some horse-rustling and sold them to the army. Settlers used to see him run horses, freight beef by night, come back with a wagonload of pelts. But he always had a good story for them, and since he was the Indian agent, nobody thought more of it. Then somewhere he made a mistake and the government nailed him. A lot of people came forward to testify then that they'd seen him pulling off his schemes. They packed him off to a federal prison back East."

Fargo felt the shock spiraling through him and heard his words gasped out. "That's it. By Christ, that's it," he breathed. "That's the hate. He's filled with it, burning up inside him and now he's getting back at all of them. He's going to let the Indians pay them back for him."

Fargo paused, the monstrousness of it assaulting his thoughts. But it was all there, suddenly everything in place. "That's why he put me onto Sam Rawley, along with Major Keyser. He had me pinned down watching a decoy while he gave himself time to hit again," Fargo muttered, voicing his racing thoughts. "I knew it had to be someone who knew the patterns of the Indian. An Indian agent would have learned them, of course. Son of a bitch!" he swore as he leaped to his feet, flew into clothes. "I've got to get him, stop him before he sets it all on fire," he bit out. "If it's not already too damn late."

Clothes on, he streaked for the door, Dolly hurrying hard to keep up with him. He halted at the door, pulled her to him, dug his hands into her soft, full rear, and felt the cushioned breasts against him. "I owe for this one, Dolly," he said as he pressed his mouth on her.

"You paid in advance," she said, and grinned.

"Just a down payment. I'll be back soon as I can," he said. "Promise."

"I'm not going anywhere," she said, and he pulled away from her enveloping warmth, yanked the door open, and raced to the Ovaro. He vaulted into the saddle and sent the horse flying up the street, skidded to a halt in front of the hotel. His boots pounded hard on the stairs as he raced to the room, knocked, waited. There was no answer.

"It's me, dammit. Open up," he yelled. Only silence followed. He tried the knob, the door came open, and he stared into an empty room. He swore, frowned. The bay was hitched outside, he'd noted. He raced down the stairs, halted at the desk. "The young lady that was with me, where is she?" he asked.

"Went into the saloon, soon after you left," the man said.

"Shit," Fargo swore as he raced out and into the adjoining entrance. Stubborn thing. She insisted on showing anger and independence. His eyes swept the room, pushing through the haze of smoke. Saloon girls by the dozen but no delicate, ash-blond hair glistening across the haze. He strode to the bar and saw the bartender watch him approach apprehensively. "Ash-blond girl, came in alone. Where is she?" Fargo barked.

"Don't ask me, mister. I don't see everybody who comes in here," the bartender answered.

Fargo leaned over the bar, his eyes blue ice. "Shit you don't," he growled. "And if you don't, you'd sure as hell have seen her. She'd stand out in here like a buttercup in a swamp."

"You calling my bar a swamp, mister?" The man frowned, but there was more show than anything else in his eyes.

"No, swamps are much better," Fargo said. "Now where the hell is she?"

"Look, I don't want trouble, mister," the man said.

Fargo's arms shot out, his hands clasping the man by the shirt. He pulled and the bartender came across the bar as if he were a six-year-old. "You'll get trouble like you've never seen trouble 'less you talk fast," Fargo growled.

The bartender swallowed, felt himself held helpless in the hands of the big man with the ice-blue eyes. "She came in, sat down, ordered a drink," the man said. Fargo relaxed his grip a fraction. "Big Bud Bascomb sat down with her. She talked to him, but when he made her an offer, she told him to shove off," the bartender said. "No gal in a saloon tells that to big Bud Bascomb."

"Where is she, goddammit?" Fargo roared.

"He carried her out over his shoulder, screaming and yelling she was. He's got a tin shack across the street, white door."

Fargo let the man go, pushed him back behind his bar with one hand, and whirling, raced from the saloon. His eyes found the shack, almost directly across from the saloon, a white door and a boarded-up window alongside it, but he saw lamplight glimmer from inside through the boards. He curled his hand around the doorknob, turned slowly, and the door opened. He stepped around two crates, a pile of old clothes, halted at a room filled with boxes, broken chairs, and a big mattress. Janice lay on the mattress, her wrists bound and tied to a chair. The man was unbuttoning her shirt, taking his time, almost drooling.

Fargo paused for a moment, saw big, bearlike shoulders, a back broad as a hay wagon, and thick folds over the back of the neck.

"I told you, I'm no saloon girl. You've made a mistake," Fargo heard Janice protest, saw the terror in her eyes as he waited just outside the doorway.

"If you ain't a saloon girl, what was you doin' in the saloon?" Fargo heard Big Bud say.

"I just stopped in. I was bored in my room," Janice tried to explain.

"You ain't gonna be bored now, sweetie," the man said, and his laugh held more anticipation than meanness.

Fargo swore under his breath. Seconds counted. He'd no time to waste. He reached down, picked up one of the wooden crates, and stepped into the room with it, lifted it over his head. Big Bud

Bascomb turned and Fargo saw a fleshy face, a hint of dull-wittedness in it, big shoulders and chest but a belly that showed the effects of too much beer drinking. He brought the crate down on the man's head with all his might. It splintered, fell down over the man's shoulders, and Big Bud toppled from the edge of the mattress onto one of the broken chairs, finishing it completely.

Fargo yanked out his throwing knife, cut Janice's wrist bonds, turned to see the man pulling the mashed crate from his head, ponderously getting to his feet. Six feet, Fargo guessed, but he looked shorter because of the fat and width of him. Big Bud Bascomb let out a roar, charged like a bull elephant. Fargo ducked away from the charge, let the man thunder to a halt, turn. He shot a snapping left to Big Bud's jaw.

"Agh, shit," the man gasped out as his head snapped around and he took a step backward. Fargo's next blow was a pile driver right, delivered with all the power of his shoulders behind it. His fist went into the round, beer-glutted belly almost up to his wrist. He spun away as Big Bud's breath shot from him in a gurgling gasp and, with it, a stream of hardly digested beer that spewed fountainlike onto the floor. The big figure dropped to one knee, his mouth hanging open as he gasped for breath. Locking both hands together, Fargo brought a double-handed blow down on the back of the man's neck, and Big Bud Bascomb pitched onto his face, spewed out more beer, and lay with his face in it, moaning softly.

Fargo yanked Janice by the wrist, almost pulled her as he charged out of the shack. "Hit the saddle," he roared. "We got a lot of riding to do."

She mounted, wheeled the bay, and caught up to

him as he galloped up the main street. He glared at her. "I thought you'd stopped being a pain in the ass," he said.

"I told you I wasn't staying there alone while you were off enjoying the mayor," she returned. "I couldn't."

"You couldn't," he echoed, and she returned his glare. "Well, now, that's a promising sign," he said.

She looked away as she answered. "Why are we running off in the middle of the night like this?" she asked. "Trouble at City Hall?"

"No trouble there," Fargo said. "Plenty someplace else. Tom Benton's the one behind all of it."

Janice stared at him in disbelief. "Benton?" she gasped.

"He was an Indian agent, a bad apple all around," Fargo said, and told her what Dolly had said. "It all fits right," he said as he finished. "Hate, not just greed. Burning hate and vengeance."

"That's what I saw in those eyes," Janice murmured. "I felt it without knowing what it was, just that something terrible was there." She paused and Fargo saw thoughts turning behind her eyes. "One thing I still don't understand. You killed three raiders. Sam Rawley lost three men. That's still a pretty strange coincidence."

"A coincidence arranged by Benton. He'd planned a raid and purposely let me stop it. He was there, somewhere near, watching to see, and when I brought down three of his raiders, he hightailed it to Sam Rawley's place, with Thorst probably, and pulled off the attack on the bunkhouse."

"He sacrificed three of his men, killed three more to point the finger at Sam Rawley once and for all," Janice finished, awe in her voice.

"It damned near worked. It was damn hard to

swallow Sam Rawley's story," Fargo said. "Benton's keeping his hired guns away somewhere. Thorst is his go-between, riding out to give orders and bring the men in for each raid. Benton planned it all too well, damn his twisted soul."

"Vicky?" Janice asked.

"She's no part of it, except that he's her pa. I'd stake my neck on that," Fargo told her.

"Blood's thicker than water. I'd be careful," Janice said.

He took in her words, accepting the truth as well as the edge of waspishness in them.

Dawn began to slide its pink veil across the sky and Fargo steered the pinto closer to the edge of the timber to avoid riding out in the open. He rode with grim uneasiness draped around him as if it were an invisible cloak. Every minute counted. Maybe there was still time. Benton had had to move carefully, send Thorst to hire three men to replace the ones he'd sacrificed. Yet he'd gotten himself four days, more than enough time to strike again, more than enough time to set the prairie on fire and drench the territory in blood. Fargo cursed the man's hating, vengeance-filled soul as he raced the pinto through the heat of the morning sun.

He had just started down over a low hill when Janice called to him and he slowed. "I'm exhausted, Fargo," she said. "I've got to rest some."

"You can rest after we get to Benton's," he said.

"To Benton's?" She frowned. "That's almost a day's ride. I can't make it without some sleep."

He reined up, speared her with a harsh glance. "All right. What's a massacre to a little sleep," he bit out.

"That's unfair," she said.

"Unfair's got nothing to do with it," he threw back. "All hell breaking loose has."

He saw her lips tighten and she pushed knees into the bay. "Let's ride," she snapped.

He followed, came alongside her, realized he was fast developing a new respect for Janice Davidson. Stubborn, bitchy, headstrong, she nonetheless carried her own reservoir of courage. Or maybe she was just growing up. Either way, she didn't back off when the chips were down.

He made a slow turn to stay near the line of oak, noted the pony tracks on the ground, and kept one eye on the closely banked trees, another on the distant ridges.

They'd ridden into the afternoon, just started down a slow slope near the timberline when he reined up, frowned, and Janice followed his eyes to an object barely visible at the edge of the trees. He drew the Colt, held it in his hand as he steered the Ovaro forward. The object didn't move as he drew closer, became a deerskin dress. He swung from the horse as he reached the spot, his lips drawn back as he saw the deerskin stained red. The woman's form took shape under the loose garment, black hair lying half over her face.

He knelt down, heard Janice come up as he bent closer to the woman. "She's dead," he said. He moved the red-stained dress and cursed softly. Three bullet holes pitted the top of the hide.

He got to his feet, his eyes sweeping the ground, picked up the bloodied trail on the grass. It led into the trees and he took the Ovaro's reins in hand, motioned to Janice to dismount. She followed as he moved beside the trail of blood, into the trees, saw where the woman had fallen against a stump, pulled herself up again to go on. The cold knot began to form in the pit of his stomach as he followed the trail. The woman had wandered erratically through the trees, little spots of blood turning brown on the bark of a half-dozen oaks.

Fargo halted, sniffed the air, drew in the scent of smoke. Janice, her eyes wide, nodded to him as he motioned for her to leave her horse beside the Ovaro. He went forward in a crouch, Janice on his heels, and he glimpsed the tepee through the trees, halted, listened. The absolute silence tightened the knot in his stomach and he moved forward. The camp came into full view, three tepees, a drying rack with two elk hides stretched on it, an almost-burned-out fire nearby. And strewn around the camp, like so many wooden Indian dolls, the silent, stiff figures, a half-dozen women, four kids, he counted, an old man. All had been shot, most three or four times.

"My God," he heard Janice whisper beside him.

His eyes swept the small camp again. "Arapaho," he said. "The men haven't come back yet, haven't found them. Let's get the hell away from here." He turned, strode back to the horses, saw Janice start to mount. He reached up, pulled her back. "Stay on foot," he whispered. He led the way back the way they'd come, had just reached the edge of the tree cover when he saw the line of bronzed horsemen returning as the day began to close. He sank down in the high brush beside the treeline, Janice coming against him, a soft pressure at his side. He peered at the line of braves, counted eight, four carrying freshly skinned buffalo hides. The Indians disappeared into the trees and he waited a few minutes more, rose, and swung onto the Ovaro.

"Ride," he said through gritted teeth, sent the horse racing, stayed near the trees. He halted only when he was certain he'd ridden far enough away and moved into the woods as the night swallowed the last of the day. He found a little glen, slipped out of the saddle, and stretched out on a wide bed of soft broom moss. Janice folded herself down beside him, her eyes still wide with shock. He felt the terrible weariness of defeat sweep through him.

"Too late," he muttered. "Too late. The fat's in the fire now."

8

He lay wrapped in silence, and the moon came up to sprinkle silver light through the trees. Janice waited, stayed still beside him until he heard her whispered words. "What happens now?" she asked.

"They'll wrap the dead in burial shawls, chant the night away, and go to a burial ground in the morning," Fargo told her.

"Then?" she persisted.

"Get ready to take the warpath," he said, and the bitterness was hard in his voice.

The moon rose higher and shimmered through the tree branches and the night stayed warm. "Enjoy it," Fargo murmured. "Could be the last moon you'll see, honey."

"How long before they take the warpath?" Janice asked.

"A day, maybe two," Fargo answered. "They've got to come together and there are things they'll do first, rituals, war dances, prayers to the Thunderbird."

"And Benton?" she asked.

"Probably hightailed it by now. He knows what'll happen and he won't figure to get caught in it. Bastard probably has an escape route all mapped out," Fargo said. "He'll be taking Vicky along, that's the only good thing."

"And you?" Janice pressed.

"It'll be too much of a risk trying to get you through to Kearny now," he said. "I'll get you back to Prairie Dog, that's closest. You can stay there with Dolly. There's no guarantee they won't hit there, but it's not likely."

"No," Janice said firmly.

He shot her a pained glance. "You going to give me a hard time because of Dolly?" he said.

"Nothing to do with that," Janice said, cutting him off. "I want to stay. I want to see it through with you." Fargo's frown dug into his brow as he watched her. "It was all words once, nothing more, massacre just one more word. It's not now. I understand what it means now. If there's any last chance to stop it, I want to help," Janice said.

Fargo's black brows lifted. "Making up for Daddy?" he asked.

"Guess that's part of it. You said it back then. It was selfish, wrong. I know what that meant now," she said.

His eyes stayed on her. "You might just turn out to be pretty special," he said.

"I know what a lot of other things about myself meant, too," Janice said. She leaned forward and he felt the touch of her lips, soft, gentle. She drew back. "So much is so clear all of a sudden," she said.

"Confessions?" he asked.

"No, more like admissions, mostly to myself," she said. "When suddenly there might not be any tomorrows, you see differently."

He reached a hand out, circled the back of her neck, felt the softness of her skin there, drew her to him. "Wanting is reason enough. You don't need any others," he said, and her lips parted for his mouth, sweet honey taste to her. He drew her forward, then turned with her, placed her on the soft moss. His lips opened, pulled against her mouth, pressed forward, and his tongue slipped into her, quick, darting motions. He felt the tremor go through her.

His fingers began to open the buttons of her shirt, not hurrying, and he listened to her breaths grow shallow, quicken. He opened the last button and the shirt fell open. He saw beautifully round breasts, perfectly proportioned, downy white and the areolas a pale, pale pink, the flattened nipples even pinker.

She half-rose, helped him draw the shirt from her, and he saw her eyes wide and round, staring at him as he shed clothes. He was in underpants only when he pulled her skirt free, then the undergarment, and she drew her knees up at once, an automatic gesture. He pulled them down and she gave a tiny gasp as his hand stayed on one thigh.

Fargo's gaze traveled slowly over her cream-white figure, beautifully curved abdomen, a smooth, faintly convex little belly, and beneath it, a delicate, curly blond nap. It fitted her, not ash-blond but light enough, almost matching the blond eyebrows and lashes, everything about her pastel, from the pale-pink areolas to the blond triangle. He caressed one delicately tinted nipple and Janice cried out at once, a tiny gasp. He leaned down, took her breast into his mouth, and let his tongue circle the edges of the areola, move across the small, flattened nipple. "Oh . . . oh . . . oh, God," Janice murmured as he felt the tiny tip stiffen, rise, enough for him to pull on it with his lips. He pulled, caressed with his tongue, and felt Janice move, her lips lifting, falling back, her legs turning to one side together, then to the other. He ran his fingers slowly down the center of her creamy body, circled the little belly button, and she cried out in a quick half-gasp, traced a line across her belly, pressed his fingers through the blond triangle.

"Fargo . . . please, oh, no, oh, no," he heard her whisper even as her hands tightened around his back, pressed, rubbed, entreated. He pushed down deeper into the blond nap, pressed his palm against the soft mound of Venus, held it there. "Oh, no, no," Janice breathed, and he saw her legs tighten together, entwine. He pressed down, slipped his finger over the hirsute little curve that dipped between her legs, pushed into the softness of her thighs, which stayed tight.

"Oh . . . oh, no, please . . . oh, my God," Janice murmured, words almost whispered, little lies of habit, her gasps making a mockery of denial. He reached deeper, his finger tracing its path to the wet lips, touching, holding there for a long moment. "Aaaaah . . . ah, God, oh, oh, no . . . oh," Janice cried out, and suddenly she stiffened, drew her legs up, tried to roll free of him. He brought her back roughly, slapped her legs away, kept his hand pressed to her, and his finger moved slowly, gently, stroking, parting, pushing into moist warmth.

He heard her breath suck in, her body tremble as he stroked, pushed deeper, a tender probing, found the tender inner wall and tickled. Her breath was a moan, protest, then pleasure, the moan turning into a wavering, throaty purr. "Fargo . . . oh . . . Fargo, I want," she whispered, as if ashamed to say the words aloud.

She drew her knees up again, but this time her cream-white legs fell open, closed at once, fell open again. He came over her, rested his hot, throbbing organ across her blond bush, and her hands dug into his back. He felt her draw back on the ground, a kind of shrinking away, and he moved slowly, gently, rested his eager maleness at the dark, warm threshold.

"Ah ... iiiieee ... oh, please, easy ... easy ..." Janice gasped. He moved in slowly, slid into her wet darkness, softly enveloping, felt his size pushing open her sweet softness. She cried out, a sharp gasp, then the throaty purr once again, the sound rising and falling as he began to move inside her. Her arms reached up, circled his neck, drew him down onto her breasts, and he sucked the pale-pink tips. She suddenly seemed to laugh, a short gasp of joyful pleasure. "Fargo, Fargo ... oh, yes, wonderful ... wonderful," she whispered against his ear. Slowly Janice began to move her hips back and forth, long, sliding motions, drawing him in and away, in and away, sensuous yet delicate, tiny murmurs of pleasure coming from her lips with each long surge.

No practiced art, he knew, only her own natural sensuality surging to the surface as she drew back and forth with him, reveling in the slow ecstasy of the flesh within flesh, the juncture of throbbing, pulsing touch. She had just drawn him in when he felt her tighten around him and her eyes snapped open, almost in panic. "Oh! Ah, ah ... oh, God," Janice cried, half-screamed. "It ... it's coming ... I'm coming ... oh, my God, oh, God." The panic stayed in her wide-eyed stare as her body responded, took command of all senses, overwhelmed, consumed, frightened. He felt her tightening around him, tiny pressures of pleasure.

He slid deep as he felt her cream thighs draw tight around him, her pubic mound lift, push hard against him, and her blondness grew pink, as pale a pink as her tiny nipples and areolas. The throaty purr came again, spiraled into a deep cry, the edge of panic overwhelmed by pleasure, and she gave sudden little shuddering pumping motions as the climax coursed through her.

Her sigh was drawn from deep inside as the hanging moment of pure ecstasy vanished, almost as suddenly as it had seized her. She dropped back onto the cool moss, her body still infused in pale pink. "So quick, so quick," she murmured in protest, held him to her, and cried out as he kissed the creamy breasts, her hands running through his thick black hair. He lay over her, finally drew from her, and met her eyes, a kind of disbelief in their hazel depths. "What do I say now?" she murmured.

"No need for saying," he told her.

"I feel as though I ought to say thank you," Janice said. "Silly, isn't it?"

He laughed, cupped a hand around one creamy breast. "You said it already," he told her.

She frowned in thought, her eyes somber as she studied him. "Somehow, I don't think it would have been as wonderful with someone else," she said.

"You'll never know that now," he answered.

She turned, stretched on her back, turned again, lay half over him. "It *was* wonderful, Fargo, wonderful and strangely scary at the end, as though some part inside of me was running away with all of me."

His eyes sought the moon through the ceiling of leaves, saw it had moved halfway down the trackless path in the sky. "The night's still young," he said. "Time to run away with yourself again."

"Yes," she breathed. "I'd like that." Her eyes held on him, suddenly somber. "So much to learn, so little time left," she said.

"We'll make the most of it," he said, took her hand, moved it down, placed her palm over the warm, resting shaft.

She gave a tiny gasp, started to draw her hand back, stopped, closed her fingers around him. She nodded against him. "Nice," she breathed. "Nice."

He let her explore, probe, gather new pleasures to herself, and when the moon had carried itself far down the sky, her cry had no more panic in it, only the sound of pure joy. She turned against his side, held herself close to him, and slept, satisfied, content in a way she had never been before. He closed his eyes, slept with her cradled in his arms until the morning came, filtering fitfully down through the trees.

He rose, dressed, stood at the edge of the trees, and his eyes swept the land. Quiet, peaceful, and behind the quietude, the terrible gathering. He turned away, his mouth a thin line. He heard Janice stir and watched her sit up, creamy breasts so beautifully molded, the pale-pink areolas, everything delicate and pastel about her, from the ash-blond hair and blond brows to the almost-blond little triangle. She got to her feet, took a towel from her saddlebag, and used her canteen to wash, suddenly halted, became aware of him watching her. Her small smile carried a smugness and she stretched her lovely body, turned, almost pirouetted, finally pulled on clothes, and he understood the new enjoyment of herself.

"Wish there was more time," he said as he moved to her.

Her eyes clouded at once, grew angry. "I wish Benton could be made to pay," she said. "I know, there's no way he can be made to pay for what he's done, not really. Hanging him wouldn't make up for the lives of all those people that are going to die. That's the damn shame of it. He ought to pay, somehow, in some horrible way."

Fargo's gaze stayed on the anger, the raging indignance mirrored in her face, and suddenly he felt the thought spiraling up inside him as her words hung in the air. She paused, saw his eyes on her. "All right, I'm ranting and raving, but that's how I feel. There's no way of making him pay, really pay, and that's insult added to injury."

"Maybe," Fargo muttered, "maybe there is." Janice stared at him, a little furrow digging into her forehead. "If they'd listen. If they'd buy it," he said.

"What are you talking about?" she asked.

"Benton," he said. "And the Sioux and all the others. If I could convince them it was Benton, turn him over to them, it might be enough. It just might," he added, thinking aloud.

"What makes you think they'd listen?" Janice asked.

"I'm hoping, not thinking," Fargo said. "There's a Sioux chieftain, I gave him his life when he thought he was done for. He'll most likely be the one leading the uprising. He might listen."

"How will you get to him?" she asked.

"I know where he had his hunting camp. I'd guess it's still there, and the others will come to him," Fargo said.

"You figure to sneak in?"

"No way," he said. "That'll get me killed for sure. There's only one way to bring this off: boldness, surprise, make them stand back in wonder. I've got to ride in bold as brass."

"And if they won't believe you, won't settle for Benton?" she questioned.

His shrug was bitter. "They'll start with me," he said.

"Us," Janice corrected.

"Oh, no," he said, "there's no damn sense in you sticking your neck in this."

"There's a lot of sense," she returned. "Ride in bold as brass, you said. That's the only thing that'll do it. It'll really set them back with me beside you."

He frowned at her but couldn't deny her words. Her ash-blond loveliness beside him would be that extra stroke that would pull it off. They'd let him through, stand back in awe, that much was certain. "I'm a damn fool. You're a bigger one," he said.

"Two damn fools are better than one," she answered. "Let's go."

He pulled her to him and her mouth welcomed his lips. "For luck," he said, and she nodded. He drew back, climbed onto the Ovaro, and Janice rode out beside him as he headed back north by east. He stayed as close to tree cover as possible and the trip became one of almost as much hiding as riding. Every few miles he found himself taking cover, waiting, as lines of warriors moved across their path, all heading in the same direction.

"Word's been sent out," he muttered to Janice while they hid in a clump of sagebrush as a line of fifteen Crow wound their way across their path. When the Crow had ridden on out of sight, he led the way forward again, but the day was wearing down when he came into sight of the terraced ridges that had marked the Sioux hunting camp. He started the pinto up the first of the ridges, then the second, and halted, his eyes on Janice as the sound of war drums echoed from beyond the thick timber on the next ridge.

"Want to change your mind?" he asked.

Her eyes met his, not hiding the flash of fright that had seized her. "I want to, but I'm not going to," she said, and moved her horse forward.

He grunted, admiration in the sound, and led the way into the trees, moved forward slowly as the timber thinned and the sound of the drums grew stronger. The twilight was still with them and his eyes moved back and forth ceaselessly, from the higher land on one side to the hill on the other.

He felt Janice's hand reach out, dig into his arm. "Up there," she whispered. "Two of them, watching us."

He glanced at the two Sioux warriors on the hill, smiled at her. "We passed a half-dozen more watching us," he said. "You didn't spot them."

The trees opened into a short path and Fargo slowed as a horde of bronzed bodies blocked the way. "Heads up," he muttered to Janice as he moved forward. The drums suddenly stilled and he pushed the Ovaro on. The braves moved back, their eyes full of astonishment, almost awe, as they watched the big man with the black hair and the ash-blond goddess beside him.

Fargo saw the three tepees come into sight and Two Beavers emerged from one, the wide, beaded choker still around his neck. He saw recognition come into the Indian's eyes as he halted in front of the tepee. Two Beavers peered at him, shifted his glance to Janice. Many of the others were already in warpaint, Fargo took note.

"You are very stupid or very brave," the Sioux chieftain said.

"We come in peace," Fargo said.

"You are very stupid," the Sioux decided, his black eyes flicking to Janice again, lingered on the ash-blond hair. Fargo saw the tiny beads of perspiration coating Janice's forehead. "Why did you bring her?" he asked Fargo.

"To show that I come in peace," Fargo answered.

The Sioux turned the answer in his mind, his black eyes glittering, his reply both an acceptance and a refusal. "It is too late to talk of peace," he said.

"It is never too late to talk," Fargo countered.

"The white men have raided, killed, attacked the last camp. They have taken us to the warpath," the chieftain said.

"One white man," Fargo said, and the Indian frowned. "One white man," he repeated. "Not the others. Only one who wanted to see this happen." Fargo glanced at the other warriors clustered in a circle around him.

"Lies," one called out.

Fargo brought his eyes back to the Sioux chieftain. "Listen to my words. I can ask that favor of Two Beavers," he said, and knew the Sioux would understand the unsaid.

The Indian nodded slowly.

"This is not a time to take the warpath. Soon the ground will be cold. It will be time for the white winds. This is the time to prepare, to gather in food and hides, not to take the warpath. The soldiers wait. You will kill many, but you will lose many, those young hunters you need to prepare for the hard days." He paused, tried to find a reaction in the Indian's face, but the man waited impassively. "I will bring this man to you, give him to you," Fargo said. "The one who has tried to bring you to the warpath."

He drew a deep sigh, waited. He had thrown his ace card. White man didn't turn their own over to the Indians. It was an offering too often asked and never given. He caught the surprise in the Sioux chieftain's black eyes, sat back in the saddle, held his breath.

The Indian swept the others circled around him with a long glance, finally returned his gaze to the big man with the lake-blue eyes. "You will give us one of your own to punish?" he questioned, wanting to hear the offer again.

"I will do this. I speak only for myself. But I will do this. He is the guilty one, not all the others. Do not take the warpath. I will give him to you," Fargo said.

The Sioux's glittering black eyes took on narrowed shrewdness. "How do we know this is not a trick?" he asked. "How do we know that you are not only trying to make time to bring more soldiers?"

Fargo felt his lips bite down on each other; the question speared hard and he'd no proof to give, no more than words with which to answer. "It is no trick," he said. "I will come back with him."

The Sioux looked away and Fargo saw him turning the offer and the answer in his mind. The Indian's eyes came back, narrowed, glitteringly hard, slowly moved to Janice. "She stays," he said. "You bring him back to us and you can go with her. If this is a trick, if you do not return with this man, she dies. You will have two moons."

Fargo kept his face expressionless as the thoughts circled wildly inside him. But the circles had no end, just as he had no choice. The Sioux had met his challenge. If he refused, the Indian would surely take it as proof he had lied, had come only with tricks aimed at buying time. And if he agreed, and he couldn't find Benton to bring him back in time

... He didn't finish the question. His eyes went to Janice. "Goddamn," he swore bitterly. "Goddamn."

He saw Janice turn to him, wryness in her shrug. "We don't have a choice, Fargo," she said.

"None," he agreed grimly. "He outfoxed us. He's tossed the ball back to us."

"Run with it, Fargo," she said. "Run fast and run hard," she added fervently.

His eyes stayed on her. "I'll be back, with him or without him, but I'll be back."

She nodded, the wryness in her eyes. "You know I'll be waiting," she said.

Fargo turned to the Sioux chieftain, his eyes ice-crystals, and the Indian read his thoughts. "She will be safe for two moons," he said.

Fargo nodded, leaned over in the saddle, and Janice's mouth opened for his kiss. He drew back after a moment. "Don't be afraid," he said as he turned the Ovaro and slowly started to ride from the camp. The circle of hostile faces parted to let him through and he walked the Ovaro unhurriedly, sent the horse into a gallop only when he was gone from the camp.

He raced across the terraced ridges and rode hard in the moonlight, thundering through the night. The dawn broke into the sky before he reined up at the broken-down house. He dismounted, saw the barn door open, the runabout inside, but the horses gone. He circled the house as he scanned the ground, quickly found the tracks. Three horses, he grunted. Benton, Vicky and Thorst, most likely. He climbed back onto the Ovaro, his eyes following the hoof-prints.

Benton had headed north, and Fargo cursed the man's efficient cleverness, his awareness that the tribes would mostly sweep south and west.

Fargo set the Ovaro out on a fast trot alongside the trail marks, and he'd ridden most of the morning when he realized that Benton was headed for the forested terrain just beyond Slim Buttes. The tracks told him that Benton hadn't more than a day's head start, and he increased the pinto's pace, held it until he pulled to a halt to stare down at the hoofprints. One of the horses had pulled a leg, developed a limp, the right forefoot. He smiled in grim satisfaction as he rode on. He drew up again beside a small stream where they had halted. He dismounted and saw the hoofprints, read them carefully. They'd taken the horse with the bad leg to one side, doctored him, had him standing on three legs beside a wedge of sagebrush.

Fargo rose, crossed the stream to peer at the tracks that went on. The horse still limped, but only a little now, he saw grimly. They'd bandaged the foreleg, probably a sprained pastern, he guessed as he swung back on the Ovaro. They had gone on considerably more slowly, he saw, and by the time the day drew near an end, he reckoned they weren't far ahead of him. On the horizon, he could make out the heavy forest land rising up, and he spurred the horse on, suddenly reined him to a halt to frown down at the trail. One had turned off, heading directly north, left the other two. That would be Thorst, he guessed, which left Benton riding the horse with the sprained leg. He peered after the tracks that went off, eyes narrowed, but he had no choice once again. He had to keep after Benton and Vicky.

Fargo touched the Ovaro with his knees and the horse moved forward. He concentrated on following the two sets of hoofprints before him. Benton had ridden an almost-straight line, obviously confident he wouldn't be followed. As the dark descended, Fargo speeded the pinto on as the forest rose up tall and dense in front of him. The tracks ran straight into the forest and he followed, slowed as the dark closed in around him at once, and he swore at the blackness that made tracking impossible. He dismounted, leaned back against a tree, and waited until the soft silver light filtered down to give some definition to the forest. He stared up at the almost-round white sphere in the sky. One moon, he muttered bitterly.

Tracking ground marks was impossible, and he watched for the broken ends of low branches, leaves pushed aside, crumpled, underbrush pushed down by the passage of horses. He hadn't gone too far into the heavy forest terrain when his keen nostrils caught the smell of smoke; he dismounted, moved forward on foot, glimpsed the glow of a small fire in the distance. He headed toward the flickering pale-orange light and the figure beside the fire came into view: first, Benton, the man seated, resting on one arm.

Fargo crept forward silently, halted but a few feet from the tiny fire, and his eyes sought Vicky, found her standing nearby, cleaning a tin plate. He drew the big Colt .45 as he stepped from behind the trees, the gun trained on Tom Benton.

Vicky saw him first. "Fargo," she cried out, her voice filled with surprise and delight.

Fargo watched Benton turn, the man's intense blue eyes holding a moment of surprise as he looked up. Fargo moved forward, caught Vicky's frown as she started toward him, halted as she saw the Colt in his hand.

Tom Benton's lips formed an icy smile. "Managed to stay alive, did you?" he said.

"And put it all together," Fargo rasped. "Dolly Westin remembered you when I mentioned your name. She opened it all up for me."

Tom Benton shrugged almost nonchalantly. "I figured that might happen," he said.

Vicky's voice cut in as she stepped closer. "What is all this? What are you talking about?" she frowned.

Fargo's eyes stayed on the man. "You want to tell her?" he growled.

Benton shrugged.

"Tell me what?" Vicky put in anxiously.

"That he's the one behind stirring up the Indians," Fargo bit out, saw Vicky's frown grow into instant disbelief.

"No, you don't know what you're talking about, Fargo," she said.

"Don't I?" Fargo said, his eyes staying on Tom Benton. "Tell her I'm wrong, Benton," he said.

Vicky turned to stare at her father. The man didn't look at her, stayed motionless, eyes on the big Colt.

"Those three years he disappeared, he was in a federal prison," Fargo said. "He was an Indian agent, a stinking, rotten, thieving one, until they caught up to him."

He saw Vicky stare at her father, the disbelief still clinging to her face. "He's all wrong, isn't he?" she asked. "It's all a mistake, isn't it?"

The man slowly turned to look at her. "No mistake," he said. He started to say more when his body shook and the racking cough seized him. Fargo watched him as the cough shook him for perhaps two minutes, finally subsided, and Tom Benton's intense eyes turned to his daughter. "Got these lungs in their goddamn jail, cold, rotten, vermin-infested place. They just left me to cough myself to death till I broke out," he said, his voice gathering fury. He turned, half-rose, the intense blue eyes blazing venom. "And all those good settlers who helped put me there, now they'll pay for it," he flung out.

Vicky continued to stare in shock at him, her mouth hanging open. "Pa, Pa, what have you done?" she murmured.

"I've done what I planned to do those three years in their rotten jail, pay them back, all of them, pay them back," the man snarled.

Fargo spoke to Vicky as he kept the Colt trained on her father. "He robbed, cheated, swindled his own government and the Indians he was supposed to see after. Now he's a madman and hundreds, maybe thousands, of innocent men, women, and children will die because of him."

The man kept his intense eyes on his daughter. "I made myself some extra money and I sent most of it to you and your ma. Couldn't have sent it if I didn't steal some," he said.

"Bullshit," Fargo said.

Tom Benton turned to him and his smile was sudden, full of craftiness. "You can kill me, Fargo, but that won't stop it, not anymore. You can't stop it, Fargo," he said triumphantly.

"You can stop it," Fargo said. "The Sioux and the others will settle for you, Benton."

The man frowned, stared at him. "What are you trying to pull off?" he asked.

"I'm bringing you back to them," Fargo said, threw a quick glance at Vicky. She stared at him now, dark eyes round with shock.

"What kind of shit are you trying to hand me?"

Benton said, but Fargo caught the edge of uncertainty in his voice.

"No shit, Benton. They're waiting for you. I told them I'd give you to them," Fargo answered.

"You'd turn me over to those murdering, torturin' savages?" The man frowned.

"Wouldn't lose a second's sleep over it," Fargo answered.

Tom Benton uttered a harsh laugh. "Only you're not turning me over to anybody," he said.

"You heard the man," the voice cut in from behind him, and Fargo stiffened, his finger hardening on the trigger until he pulled it back. "Drop the gun," the voice said.

9

"Better do as Hank says." Benton smiled.

Fargo's glance found Vicky. She stared, seemed transfixed in shock. "Drop the damn gun," he heard Thorst snarl, and he swore silently as he let the Colt slip from his fingers. Thorst hadn't left when his tracks veered north. He'd headed off and then turned to ride parallel. Tom Benton's words underscored his bitter realization.

"Didn't really expect you following us, Fargo, but I'm a cautious man. I believe in covering every possibility. When it started to get dark, I sent Hank off to ride backup." Benton smiled. "Extra care always pays off." Fargo saw the man's smile vanish, his intense eyes blaze as he turned to Thorst. "Get rid of him. Shoot him," he snapped.

"No!" Fargo heard Vicky cry out. "Hasn't there been enough killing. You can tie him up, leave him."

"Leave him to maybe get loose with what he knows?" Her father frowned. "Never. You just stay back."

Fargo heard the exchange dimly, faintly, as if from a great distance, his thoughts on round hazel eyes that trusted, on all those for whom his death would be the final epitaph. He swore silently, refused to go down without a final effort.

"No, please," he heard Vicky implore her father, but the man's snarl was an uncompromising refusal.

"Look the other way, dammit," Benton told her.

"Can I have a minute?" Fargo asked, dropped to one knee, and saw Benton's icy smile.

"You're full of surprises, Fargo," Benton sneered.

"A man's got a right to pray," Fargo said, bowing his head.

"Make it fast," Benton rasped.

Fargo stayed with his head bowed. Thorst was behind him to his right, Benton off to the side as his hand stole up the leg of his trouser, drew the double-edged throwing knife from its leather holster around his calf. Keeping his head bowed, he flicked a glance at Thorst. The distance, the timing, the angle, everything was all wrong, and yet it was his last chance. He couldn't try for accuracy, only surprise. He half-turned, as if starting to rise to his feet, flung the knife underhanded, the thin blade hurtling through the air.

Thorst saw it come at him, his reaction automatic. He twisted away as he fired, the shot going wild. The knife hit him sideways on the shoulder, bouncing harmlessly away, but Fargo was diving into the brush, rolling, rolling again, as two shots went over his head. He heard Benton cursing as he crouched in the thick brush.

"Take that side, I'll take the other," Benton ordered. "Kill the son of a bitch."

Fargo watched the two figures start to move through the trees from opposite sides, outlined by the faint glow of the fire behind them. Though weaponless, facing a desperate madman and an icy hired killer, he managed a grim smile. He still held an advantage, perhaps small yet invaluable. They were no hunters. They knew how to chase but not to hunt. They advanced, confident in their guns, certain their quarry was helpless, able only to hide. Fargo backed deeper into the forest, using the noise they made to cover his movement. One thing remained vital: Benton had to be kept alive. The Sioux chief would not accept a lifeless body. That would be a meaningless offering that denied them their own revenge. Benton had to be turned over alive, Fargo repeated, which meant that for now the man had to be immobilized while he dealt with Thorst.

Fargo cast a quick glance through the trees at the fire, saw Vicky standing with her hands lifted to her mouth, staring into the darkness. He dropped low, let his hands grope along the forest floor, felt the smooth stems of wood fern, the capsules of urn moss, passed over a half-dozen clusters of common inky caps, finally stopped, closed around a rock that was small, yet enough for what he needed.

Benton's snarl came through to him and he saw the two men had converged. "He's gone in deeper. He's laying low," the man said. "He's got to be close."

Fargo stayed motionless as the two figures started toward him. He waited, pushed himself silently to his feet, stayed behind the trunk of an elm, his hand closed around the small rock. The two men moved closer and he stepped from behind the tree, drew his arm back, took aim, waited a few seconds more, and then hurled the rock.

He saw it slam into Benton's temple, heard it land and the man's short cry of pain as he fell. Fargo dived to the ground as Thorst fired, two shots that whistled over his head. He rolled, hit the nearest tree trunk with the side of his hand, and Thorst fired another shot, the sixth including those he'd fired when the knife had struck him.

Fargo leaped to his feet, charged forward, and Thorst, starting to reload, saw him coming. He brought the gun up, used it as a tomahawk might be used, swung the barrel in a sharp arc. Fargo pulled back as the gun grazed his face, tried a quick blow, but Thorst spun away, brought the gun barrel around in a backhand swipe. Again, Fargo just managed to duck the blow, but this time he came in low, a quick tackle that caught the man at the knees and sent him toppling backward.

Fargo released his hold to swing an upward blow, and he received a kick full on the shoulder that made him wince in pain, fall aside. Thorst leaped to his feet, the gun still in his hand. He brought the weapon down in a hammerlike blow, and Fargo rolled his head aside as the gun slammed into the ground. He spun back, hit Thorst's arm as he kicked out, his boot catching the man in the leg. Thorst went down, cursed, spun again. The man was quick, Fargo swore as he pulled back from the blow of a heel, regained his feet, and came at Thorst. He saw the man lash out with a left hook, parried the blow, countered with a right to the solar plexus.

Thorst grunted, a swish of breath rushing from his mouth. Fargo brought up a quick, short left that caught the man alongside the jaw. Thorst staggered back a pace, his head spinning to the side. Fargo's right came up in a driving blow, aimed at the man's solar plexus again, and with a gasp of pain, Thorst doubled over, toppled forward. Fargo's knee came up, connected with the man's jaw, and Thorst collapsed at his feet, unmoving.

Fargo turned, heard Benton's groan, and saw the man struggling to his feet. He was beside him in two long strides, yanked the gun from his holster, and flung it away. He seized Benton by the collar and dragged him back to the almost-extinguished fire, flung him to the ground. He watched Vicky rush to her father, kneel down beside him. Benton lifted his head, his eyes open. His temple had begun to swell with a small bruise and Fargo scooped the Colt from the ground, retrieved his throwing knife.

"On your feet," he barked, and Vicky helped her father up. Fargo stepped to one of the horses, cut off a length of lariat, and quickly, deftly, tied Benton's hands behind him. The man's intense eyes spit hatred at him, flashed to Vicky.

"You just going to stand there, daughter?" he said.

Fargo saw Vicky's eyes on him, round with pain. "What are you going to do, Fargo?" she asked.

"Just what I said I'd do, turn him over to the Sioux," Fargo growled.

"You can't do that, Fargo," Vicky cried out. "You know what that'll mean. They won't just kill him."

Fargo's eyes were blue-steel as they met her imploring gaze. "I know what he tried to do to hundreds of innocent men, women, and kids. I don't give a damn what they do to him. He tried to set the world on fire. He's going to burn instead."

"You bastard," Benton cursed.

Vicky's eyes stayed on the big man in front of her. "You can turn him over to Major Keyser, that's enough," she said.

"No, dammit, it's not enough. It won't stop the massacre. Turning him over to them is the only thing that'll do it," Fargo shot back.

"Don't listen to him, Vicky," Benton cut in. "Come stand here beside your pa."

Fargo shot a glance at Benton. The man was

playing his role to the hilt, digging at Vicky with everything he could bring to bear. "Shut up, Benton," Fargo barked.

"Whatever I did, I did for you and your ma, just remember that, girl," Benton called, and Fargo saw the anguish in her eyes. He cast another glance at Benton, saw the man frowning at him, a sudden slyness coming into the intense eyes. "Where's the girl, Fargo? Where's Janice?" Benton asked.

"That's nothing to do with this," Fargo said, and cursed the mad cleverness of the man.

"Where is she?" Benton repeated, and Fargo saw Vicky's eyes on him, waiting.

"The Sioux have her," he said. "They're holding her till I bring him back."

Vicky's eyes hardened at once. "Is that it, Fargo? You're bringing him back because of her?"

"Of course that's it, girl," Benton cried out.

Fargo met Vicky's stare. "It'd be the same, whether they had her or not," he bit out.

"Don't believe him, Vicky. Don't let him crucify your pa," the man argued.

Fargo's eyes stayed hard. "You've no choice, Vicky, just as I've no choice. It's his stinking hide or the lives of maybe thousands of people. There's no other way, no other choice," he said. He turned from her, took Tom Benton by the arm, and propelled him to his horse. He whistled and the Ovaro came through the trees a moment later. Fargo boosted Tom Benton into the saddle, turned to see Vicky had sunk to the ground, legs folded under her, hands held to her face. He went to her and she half-turned as he knelt down beside her, her arms reaching up to circle his neck, pull him down to her.

"Don't, Fargo, please don't. He's my pa," she begged, her face against his.

"He's no good and you haven't seen him for most of your life," he answered.

"He's still my pa," she sobbed, the small breasts pressed hard against his chest.

"Go on to wherever you were heading. You'll be safe enough now," he told her, pulled her arms from around him. Her eyes were filled with tears as they implored from their silent depths. He rose, his face carved in stone. "No choice," he murmured. "No choice." He turned, swung onto the Ovaro, took the reins of the other horse in his hand, and rode from the spot at a fast trot. He cast a last glance back as he moved through the thick forest. The small figure sat beside the fire's embers, arms held to her chest. He thought he heard the sound of sobbing, but he wasn't sure as the horses crashed noisily through the underbrush.

Benton, hands tied behind his back, rode with his intense eyes glowering, and Fargo's eyes went skyward. The moon had left the night sky and on the horizon the new day had already begun to paint a thin pink line. He swore under his breath. He had but one moon left. Janice's ash-blond hair would belong to her for but one more moon. It would be close, he muttered, too damn close. He increased the pace, shot a glance at Tom Benton.

"You worked hard on Vicky, you rotten bastard," he bit out.

The man's eyes burned into his. "What'd you expect me to do, tell her to bless you?" he snarled.

"You could've told her you were taking the blame like a man. You didn't have to lean on her. She'll feel guilty the rest of her goddamn days because of you," Fargo flung back.

The man shrugged. "She'll live with it," he said harshly.

"Bastard," Fargo said. "But that's more than you will." He quickened the pace as the sun rose and finally slowed when the round red sphere had reached the noon sky. The Ovaro was a tired horse, too tired to go on without rest, and Fargo found a cluster of rocky cones, steered the horse into them, and dismounted. The tallest cone provided enough shade to escape the heat of the sun; Fargo pulled Benton from the saddle, tied his ankles, and flung him onto the ground. He took the Ovaro into the shade and stretched himself out near the horse, felt the weariness pull at him instantly. He closed his eyes, slept until the sun had drifted across the afternoon sky.

He woke, hardly rested, yet refreshed enough to go on. His first glance was at Benton. The man had pushed himself halfway along a small crevice in the rock, had gotten himself stuck, and lay there helplessly. "Like a trapped polecat," Fargo muttered. He got to his feet, examined the Ovaro's legs. No swollen pasterns or leg tendons, he saw happily. The horse whinnied, shook its head, clearly refreshed enough to go on.

Fargo pulled Benton loose from where he'd gotten himself wedged, cut the ankle ropes, and pushed the man to his horse and helped him into the saddle. "Ride, you stinking son of a bitch," he muttered as he sent the Ovaro into a fast trot. He saw the sun, estimated he'd rested some four hours. His lips drew back as he quickened the pace, sent the Ovaro streaking across the flat prairie, cursed at the slowness of the other horse.

Dusk began to tint the horizon a faint purple and he was still on the flat land. He swore again, grabbed the reins of the other horse, tried to pull the animal faster, but gave up the thought as the horse only pulled back. He slowed a little to a steady pace and the dusk enveloped the land when he reached the first of the hills with their clusters of oak and elm.

He shot a glance at Benton. The man wore a frown that dug deep into his brow and Fargo caught the beginnings of fear creeping into the intense blue eyes. The Ovaro slowed as he climbed a long hill and Fargo saw the other horse breathing hard, reined in, took the remainder of the hill at a walk. He skirted the stands of timber, moving higher, topping the hill, and starting down the other side. He was making time, but it was not enough. The night rolled away dusk and he saw the moon come into sight, bathe the land in its pale-silver hue.

The horses were laboring now, even the Ovaro. He had pushed them as hard as he could, and he slowed again, let them walk up another hill. The moon rose higher with infuriating speed and he felt his pulse quicken as he came into sight of the terraced ridges. The Ovaro sensed his excitement, picked up speed on its own, but he held back to stay with the other horse. His eyes found Benton, saw the faintest line of perspiration on the man's brow. The second terraced ridge appeared and he climbed it quickly. The last, third one lay before him. He moved toward it, had just started up its sloping rise when he heard the voice call out.

"Fargo . . . stay there, don't move," the voice said, and he reined up, saw the slender figure ride toward him from his left, the rifle trained on him.

Vicky halted a half-dozen yards from him. "Hands on your head, Fargo," she said, and he obeyed. He heard Benton's triumphant laugh.

"That's my girl," the man said.

"I'm sorry, Fargo," Vicky said. "I followed you,

166

stayed far enough back, rested when you did. I thought about it over and over and over as I followed you. I can't let you do this. I can't let my pa be turned over to them."

"Don't do this, Vicky," Fargo said. "Leave it be. It's not your fight, not your fault." His eyes held on the rifle. It stayed unwavering. "You're condemning thousands of people to death," he said. "Because of him?"

"He's my pa," she said simply. "Good or bad, he's my pa."

Fargo cursed silently and Janice's words circled inside him. "Blood is thicker than water."

"Goddammit, he deserves what he'll get," Fargo flung out angrily, but he saw Janice's eyes were almost dulled. She was beyond reaching, inner pain and anguish forming its own impenetrable shield around her.

"Don't move, Fargo," she said as she circled her horse around behind him. He debated reaching for the Colt, but with his hands atop his head he knew he'd never make it in time.

"Untie me, honey," he heard Benton call out gleefully.

Vicky was behind him now and he heard her horse move closer. The blow caught him on the back of the head, the heavy rifle stock a most effective club. He toppled from the Ovaro to lie facedown on the ground. He heard voices, tried to move, but couldn't. The world was dark, a purple haze, the voices fuzzy and dim. Vicky's voice came through suddenly, a sharp cry that managed to become clear. "No, I won't let you," he heard her say, and the other voice was only a muffled sound. The voices faced away and he lay in stillness, fought to cling to a thread of consciousness, but the thread broke and he lay still.

He felt himself wake, felt his fingers clutching at the ground. He lifted his head, grimaced at the sharp pain that ran down the back of his neck. He opened his eyes, shook his head again, and the world took on focus, became shapes, forms, became a terraced ridge.

"Goddamn," he swore softly, his eyes on the ridge. So near and so far now. All for nothing. He pulled himself to his feet. The Ovaro stood nearby and he felt for his Colt. It was gone. Benton had taken it. He looked back through the night. He could catch up to them, but without a gun there was every chance Benton could finish what Vicky had stopped him from doing. Her words through his semiconsciousness returned, their meaning clear now. And perhaps Vicky would finally turn on him. She was determined not to let her father be turned over to the Indians. Fargo's eyes were narrowed in thought as he peered back through the night. Benton would head straight back the way they'd come, try to get as far away as he could before he'd have to stop to rest the horses. And untold people were condemned to die.

Fargo pulled himself onto the Ovaro. Once again, he had no choice. It would take him too long to catch up to them, the Ovaro too exhausted to make up time. But fresh horses could do it fast. The facts, bitter, searing facts, stabbed into him. He had no choice, he repeated as he spurred the Ovaro forward, over the last terraced ridge and down toward the Sioux camp. He saw the sentries rise as he rode into the camp, the others begin to surge forward. He galloped to the chief's tepee and slid from the saddle as Two Beavers emerged with

Janice. She looked none the worse for wear, he saw, her eyes wide with apprehension as she saw he was alone.

"You have failed," the Sioux chieftain intoned. "We listen to no more stories."

"No stories," Fargo said. "He was with me. He got away just beyond the ridge. My horse is too tired. Your warriors can catch him and bring him back." The Sioux stared, considered for a moment, turned, barked commands, and Fargo saw a dozen bucks leap onto their ponies. "He rides with a woman beside him," Fargo said.

"Bring him back alive," Two Beavers called.

"And the woman. She is innocent. She has done no wrong," Fargo said. The dozen or so warriors streaked from the camp and the others moved away. The Sioux gestured for Fargo to sit beside Janice, three tall braves coming up to stand guard as he disappeared into his tepee.

"What happened?" Janice said. "You look done in."

"Vicky came after me," he said. "I never figured she would. She took him away from me."

"What if they don't find them?" Janice asked.

"We're back to where we started. But they'll find them," Fargo said.

Janice's eyes searched his face. "You're hurting for having sent them," she said.

He nodded. "There was nothing else left, but that doesn't make me feel any better for it," he said.

"They want him. You told them she was innocent. Maybe they'll let her go," Janice said.

His lips formed a thin line and he gave a bitter sound. "Won't happen that way," he said.

Janice moved, rested against him, and the soft warmth of her body felt good. He leaned his head against her, closed his eyes. The waiting seemed forever and he lifted his head once to scan the sky, saw that the moon had moved toward the horizon, and he rested against Janice again.

He heard the sounds of the hoofbeats first, his head snapping up. He rose, pulled Janice to her feet as the Sioux chieftain stepped from the tepee. The racing horsemen came into sight, rode to a halt with Benton, an arrow in his shoulder. The man's eyes found him. "Bastard," he spat out. "No-good son-of-a-bitch bastard."

Fargo walked to the man, yanked his Colt out of Benton's belt. His eyes searched past him, into the other returned warriors, and saw only the Indian horsemen. He asked the question with the answer already curled inside him in a bitter ball at the pit of his stomach. "The girl?"

"She fought," one of the Sioux said. "She would not let us take him. She is dead."

Fargo stepped back, his eyes blue steel. "Get off the horse," he said to Benton. The man dismounted, no fear in his eyes now, only the twisted madness. He took a step toward the big man. Fargo swung, a tremendous blow with all his remaining strength behind it. It caught Benton on the point of the jaw, knocked him a half-dozen feet. Fargo turned to the Sioux chief. "He's all yours," he said.

He pulled himself onto the Ovaro and one of the braves brought the dark bay to Janice. The Sioux chieftain stepped forward, his eyes on the big man in the saddle. "I will keep my word. We will not take the warpath," he said, paused. "But there will be other times, other warpaths. You know this. I know this."

Fargo nodded and the Sioux stepped back. Janice brought the bay alongside him as Fargo wheeled the Ovaro, started from the Indian camp. Once again, the hostile, bronzed faces moved back to let him through, and he rode slowly, holding Janice back as he saw her want to race away. The moon had left the sky as they reached the terraced ridge and started down. Janice's voice came to him, almost a whisper. "You did it, Fargo. You did it," she said.

"We did it," he said.

"What now?" she asked as the day came up.

"Want to do something first," he said, and she heard the grim flatness in his voice and understood.

The sun had come up to sweep the hills with its gold when they reached the spot, the small, slender form lying on the ground. Janice reined up, stayed back as Fargo dismounted, lifted Vicky in his arms, and carried her to a cluster of bushes nearby. He saw her rifle half in the brush as he put her down, paused to pick it up. It hadn't been fired and he cursed bitterly. He used the butt end of the stock as a shovel in the soft earth, dug a shallow grave, placed the slender form in it, and covered it with dirt, branches, and a cross of small stones.

He turned, started toward Janice, and halted. The three bronzed, near-naked figures on horseback stood silently just behind her. She had neither seen nor heard them, but she turned to follow his eyes and gasped in surprise. Two of the Indians had their bows trained on him as Fargo walked forward. The third one moved down toward him, halted beside Janice, and the other two followed but kept their bows trained.

"We take her," the one said, gestured to Janice.

"Two Beavers promised we could go in peace," Fargo said.

"We are Arapaho. He did not speak for us," the Indian said. He was short, a heavy, thick body and a head to match.

"He spoke for all there. You are breaking his word," Fargo told him.

The Arapaho shrugged. "The white raiders killed our squaws. We are taking her. We have watched her for two days and two nights. We want her," he said. "Take your gun out, drop it," he said. For emphasis, he drew a hunting knife, held it into Janice's back.

Her eyes were wide with fear. "I thought they kept their word," she said to Fargo.

"They do," he said. "But there are bad apples everywhere. These are three of their kind."

"Your gun," the Arapaho barked, and Fargo drew the Colt from its holster, dropped it on the ground. One of the others lowered his bow, scooped the gun up, rode to the Ovaro, and took the reins. Fargo saw the short, chunky one's order in his eyes before he barked it to the other two, and he dived, rolled, regained his feet, and started to race for the trees as the arrows slammed into the ground. He ran in a zigzag pattern, dived into the trees as two more arrows missed him by inches. He crouched, saw the three Arapaho turn away, the short one's hand curled into Janice's ash-blond hair. They were going on. They had his horse, his gun, and Janice. They didn't much care about him.

But they hadn't seen Vicky's rifle by the bushes. Fargo ran to it, scooped it up, dropped to one knee, and aimed. He took the one holding Janice by the hair as he rode uphill, fired, and heard Janice scream as the Indian pulled on her hair as he toppled backward over the rump of his horse. The other two halted, turned. Fargo's second shot blew one

172

from his horse. The other dived into the trees and Fargo raced across the open land, saw Janice slide from her horse and crouch down.

He darted into the treeline, moved up the slope, and his ears caught the rustle of brush just ahead. He paused, listened, and the sound came again. He stepped forward, caught movement to his left, dropped flat as the arrow embedded itself in the tree behind him. He rose, saw the Indian charging toward him, tomahawk in his hand. Fargo brought the rifle up, fired almost point-blank, and the Arapaho quivered in midair, his insides spilling out. Fargo had to jump backward as the figure fell facedown at his feet. He straightened, drew a deep breath, turned the Indian onto his back, and took the Colt from his thong belt. He stepped from the trees and Janice came against him.

"God, is there no end?" she breathed.

"It's over," he said. He helped her back on the bay and led the way down the hillside, rode till the sun was high and he found a place beside a stream. He dismounted, stretched out on the grass, and she came beside him.

"Fort Kearny?" she asked, and he nodded.

"Could be a slow trip," he said. "I want to circle back, tell Major Keyser it's over."

"Good," she said. "We can combine things."

His smile was slow. "Thought you were against that," he said.

"Not if you combine the right things," she said, pressed close to him. He nodded agreement. He'd definitely combine the right things, he promised himself as he cupped his hand around one cream-soft breast. Besides, he'd earned a reward. He sighed, closed his eyes. Fort Kearny would stay a long way off.

The land grew still, peaceful, but he heard the Sioux chieftain's words linger inside him: "There will be other times, other warpaths. You know this. I know this," words that were a truth of this untamed frontier. Life and death hung on thin threads in this land. So did pleasure and pain. You learned to take each to the fullest. He slid his hand into Janice's shirt, around the sweet softness of her breasts. It was time for pleasure. The pain would wait its time.

LOOKING FORWARD

**The following is the opening section
from the next novel in the exciting
Trailsman series from Signet:**

**The Trailsman #27:
BLOODY HERITAGE**

---

*The Wyoming Territory, early 1860s,
where the land was as wild as the men
who fought and died on it.*

In the crisp forenoon the tall broad-shouldered
man with the lake-blue eyes rode the big black-and-
white pinto up the long coulee and abruptly drew
rein. Below him the lush meadow stretched to the
creek lined with cottonwoods and alders. About
halfway across, two canvas-topped wagons had
halted, while toward them rode a half-dozen horsemen at full gallop.

Skye Fargo's eyes narrowed at those pushing
riders. Something in the way they rode—loose in
their saddles, red-faced, shouting as they forced
their horses over the soft ground—told him they
were bad news. Swiftly he drew the Ovaro back
down the far side of the draw, dismounted, and
ground-hitched him, and in another moment had
stationed himself in the protection of some chokecherry bushes from where he had a clear view of

the scene below. The six riders were just yanking their sweating mounts to a jarring halt a few yards in front of the two wagons.

At that same moment a wiry, pigeon-breasted man wearing a derby hat, with gartered shirtsleeves and bright-red galluses, stepped down from the driver's seat of the lead wagon. Fargo was close enough to hear the loud greeting of the big lead rider on the steel-dust horse.

"Johnson, by God, if it ain't Mr. Kite Johnson himself in person!" And the barking laugh was instantly picked up by his companions, the roar of their high spirits sweeping up to the chokecherry bushes where the Trailsman's lake-blue eyes had turned to blue quartz as he noted the handguns in tied-down leather, the Winchesters in their saddle scabbards, and the loose arrogance with which the six sat their heaving animals. It was obvious that they'd been drinking.

"Johnson, come on over and greet your visitors," shouted a second rider, a man wearing a brown bandanna around his thick neck. He was standing up in his stirrups scratching himself as he snapped out the words, his big orange-colored face gleaming with laughter. The other men joined his guffaw, yanking their horses' mouths unnecessarily, spitting, their eyes combing the wagons, which showed no signs of life other than the two teams of horses standing still looking at the visitors. It suddenly crossed Fargo's mind that it might be a lynching.

The little man with the derby hat had just taken a step toward the six horsemen when Fargo's searching eyes caught a movement at the opening of the second wagon. It was a quick movement, yet clearly revealed a blond head of hair over a very pale face, and a bare and thoroughly female arm and shoulder.

The roar that went up showed that the riders had seen it too.

"By God, Stacey, you told it right. We've struck gold," cried the man with the orange-colored face.

Stacey, the first speaker and obvious leader of the group, leaned forward on his saddle horn, his thick arms crossed. "Come on out, girls. You got company." Then, spitting over his horse's withers, he dropped his bloodshot eyes to the man named Kite Johnson. "Good boy, there, Kite. Good boy." And a great laughter rumbled out of him.

Kite Johnson had stepped away from the wagon, holding his arms well out from his waist to show that he was unarmed.

"You're Stacey, that right?" And Fargo caught the caution in the man's voice that was not quite fear.

"Mr. Kite Johnson, you better remember that. Dutch Stacey—remember it! Shit, Kite boy, you know me and my friends from last year when you brought your fucking auction and second-dealt me that cold-ass redhead with the one eye." And quick as a lick he drew the gun at his right hip and began firing at the ground right at Kite Johnson's feet.

The little man's narrow face turned ashen beneath the derby hat as he began to hop frantically out of the way of the bullets. Instantly the other men drew their guns and joined the fun, roaring with laughter and calling out to the wagons as terrified female faces began to appear.

At the point where Kite Johnson was ready to drop, the men stopped firing, broke their guns, and started to reload. Kite was drenched with sweat, his whole body was shaking. He barely managed to speak. "What do you want, Stacey? My God, man, I've always done right by you and your boys. How come all this? What do you want?"

"You know damn well what we want," shouted a man with a totally bald head. "We want that pussy you got loaded in those wagons. And right now!"

The group roared at this, their horses stamping now as they recovered their wind and picked up on the excitement. The teams that had been pulling the wagons, however, after looking over the newcomers, now dropped their heads to resume cropping the lush feed, harnesses jingling as they kicked at flies.

Fargo watched Kite Johnson making a tremendous effort to stay on his trembling legs, and finally the little man said, "You mean, you want to hold the auction out here?"

Stacey didn't answer him. "Get them women outside them wagons," he snapped. "We want to look 'em over."

Without turning his head, Johnson called out for the women to appear. He seemed to gather strength in giving the order.

Fargo's eyes brightened with curiosity while a roar of welcome sprang from the throats of the horsemen as some dozen women began to climb down from the two wagons. Fargo was surprised to see that they were young and some were even rather good-looking.

Kite Johnson repeated his question. "You want the auction now, then?"

Stacey grinned down from his big steel-dust horse.

"Figured we would save all of us time and trouble with you not having to go through all that auctioneering business."

"No trouble," Kite said quickly, almost stammering as the visitors' plan began to unfold. "Hell, Stacey, I been running my auctions six, seven years now. Always offer the best product and never had no complaints. These lovely women"—and Fargo caught the purr that entered his voice as he stepped into his role—"why they come from far away as Boston, Philadelphia. Good families. San Francisco, that little girl over there; and that young lady with the red hair, her family, one of the fanciest in Chicago. I go to a whole lot of trouble collecting these brides-to-be for this woman-starved country, let me assure you." Kite Johnson had suddenly swept right out of his fear and timidity, and supported by his thoroughly rehearsed pitch, he seemed even to increase in size and certainly, so Fargo noted, in vibration. He was almost quivering with energy as he extolled the virtues of his ". . . young ladies from the very best families, who would make any red-blooded man a wife and mother of his children of which he would forever be proud. Why, if I say so myself, do you know any other such benefactor who finds young ladies good, virile husbands, and for you, pioneering Americans, strong-loined wives? Who else, I say, offers such a prime, essential service? And at small remuneration to myself, let me add."

Dutch Stacey and his friends were chuckling with real pleasure at the performance, and now, as Kite paused in his peroration, Stacey's big head began wagging from side to side.

"Kite, boy . . . forget the auction. We are here so's we can cut all that bullshit and just like to skim off some of the cream. You understand?"

Kite Johnson's face turned red, then gray at the thought of ruination of his auction. "But I won't have enough left for an auction if you men bid on them here—I mean, like when we get to Washing Springs."

"Kite, my friend, you don't get me even yet. There ain't going to be no auction, no bidding. We are just, like, helping ourselves."

The charged pause fell like a knife into the tableau, and for several moments, Kite, the women, the six riders, and even the horses, it seemed, waited in a quivering silence in the gleaming meadow.

"That will ruin me," Kite Johnson said softly.

"Tough."

"And it'll ruin my girls."

"Fuck the girls."

"And by God, ain't that the idea," roared someone, and the whole group joined his wild laughter.

Meanwhile the girls were out of the wagons and had lined up behind Kite, their "benefactor." Fargo had a clear view of them. They were tense, fearful; yet with some the moment seemed to emphasize certain aspects that he found attractive—fear sharpened them, changed their usual tempo, showed in one's defensive posture, in another's defiance, or even in a pleading look, each reacting in her own way to the bizarre moment.

Stacey was leaning partly out of his saddle, holding his hand out toward one of the riders, who was passing a bottle. "Kite, you and me just know those girls never seen any town east of the Mississippi nor west of the Tetons. You're full of shit with that Boston, 'Frisco talk!" He grabbed the bottle, tilted it into his jaws, allowing some to run down his chin and into his shirt. Gasping, he passed it back, easy, laughing. And suddenly the gun was in his hand and he wasn't laughing any longer.

"The boys will look over the merchandise and tell Harold here which one they're wanting." And he threw his thumb at the man with the brown bandanna and orange-colored face.

"I want that one on the end," a tall, narrow-faced man said.

"So do I," Harold barked, glaring at the man who had spoken.

Stacey was chuckling, the six-gun still in his hand. "Wrong. Both you fellers got it wrong. That one is Stacey's." And he grinned, revealing a gap where two lower teeth were missing.

Fargo's eyes had spotted the young girl standing slightly apart from the others. She stood defiantly, her head thrown back, her full bosom high and clearly outlined beneath the tight shirt. She wore tight trousers, and his eyes slipped over her loins and legs admiringly, saw that she was a lot more than mere addition; she had an air, a sparkle in her eyes, a grace when she made even the slightest move. Her dark-brown hair, swept back from a high, full forehead, emphasized widely spaced eyes. And her mouth was wide, the lips full and mobile. She was, he decided, damned good-looking.

The other men were rapidly announcing their preferences and a couple of arguments were brewing.

"How about some bids to settle it?" Kite Johnson,

stepping back into his auctioneer role, made one more attempt to salvage the financial wreckage.

Fargo's instinct, that inner voice he knew so well, was ringing through him. It was the instinct that had saved him more times than he could count: an animal, feeling thing, of nature, certainly part of his Cherokee heritage. And it called him now.

He saw her start to move even before she could have known it herself, her body tightening, a kind of charge seemed to suffuse her. And he was already bounding back over the lip of the coulee, grabbed the Ovaro's reins, stepped into the saddle, and all in a single, singing movement was up and racing over the top of the rise, the shouts tearing up from the men below as the girl ran toward the wagons. Nobody seemed to notice the big man galloping down on the big black-and-white horse. The girl was just reaching the nearest wagon, her hair flying with the riders nearly on top of her.

Fargo, kicking the Ovaro into a super effort, suddenly let out a bloodcurdling scream that sounded as though an entire tribe of Indians was on the attack. And it served its purpose. The paralyzing shock it brought gave him the seconds he needed as he charged into their midst. With the barrel of his .45 he struck Harold across his back, knocking him right out of his saddle, and without a break in rhythm, slammed Dutch Stacey on his gun arm. A third man was just lifting his own handgun to fire when Fargo, not close enough to strike him, pulled the trigger of the big Colt. The bullet, smashing into the rider's shoulder, spun him in his saddle, and he fell, screaming more with rage than pain in a tangle of reins and curses while his horse, shorn of its rider, swept on.

The girl had reached the wagon and was about to pull herself up as Fargo, swerving the Ovaro, reached down to grab her, the other riders almost on top of him. Desperately, the girl tried to pull away, not realizing he wasn't one of the gang, but his grip was secure as he seized her under the arms and dragged her up and across the pommel of his saddle. Her shirt ripped almost completely in two, and one snow-white breast sprang almost into his face as he shoved her facedown across his horse, while she kicked and screamed in rage, trying to turn to rake her nails across his eyes.

"Goddammit, I'm trying to help you," he snapped at her. But she was too far gone in her fear and fury to listen, as he turned the big horse, smashing the Colt this time at a rider who had fired so close to his head he felt the heat of the bullet passing with only the width of a playing card between himself and death. Reaching down, he grabbed the rider's boot, yanked with all his strength, and unseated him, flipping him over the other side of his horse.

The effort almost cost Fargo his own balance and he came within an ace of losing the girl, only just managing to keep her on the horse by grabbing her between her legs and pinning her. With his big hand reaching into her crotch from the rear, he held her fast, his fingers and palm tight as steel on her anus and vagina.

She kept trying to kick, but his crotch hold allowed only small movements of her legs. When she bit his leg, he tightened his grip like a vice while she screamed curses at him.

For an instant she was content, screaming, "You fucking bastard."

"Relax and enjoy it, honey. Too bad you've got these damn trousers on."

He had turned the big pinto and now they raced back across the meadow and up the long slope down which he had ridden only moments before. Shots cut the air all around them, but surprise and the decisiveness of each of the Trailsman's moves had given him the advantage as the gang lined out in pursuit, the big Ovaro, even while carrying a double load, stretching the distance.

Fargo knew it couldn't last. Even the Ovaro couldn't keep up such a pace. But he had already made his plan, and in a matter of moments, with shots still cutting too close, with the girl raging under his determined grip, they reached the top of the slope and raced down into the draw straight toward a stand of cottonwoods he'd ridden through hardly more than half an hour before.

In a moment they reached the clearing he was looking for, where sometime previously several cottonwood trees had been cut down, leaving stumps about three feet high near a stream of water. Evidently a freshet had later occurred, washing a number of fallen logs against the stumps, and so formed a small angle, making an ideal breastwork from which to fire.

"Jump," Fargo shouted at the girl, releasing her and himself sweeping out of the saddle as the big horse sped on into the trees. He landed beside the girl in a mass of debris, beautifully protected by the logs.

In seconds the riders broke into the clearing, but

Fargo had pulled the Sharps down with him and, rolling now, had come up under perfect cover, knocking the first man right out of his saddle. With the girl beside him, he found another target, the gang's bullets wasted as Fargo and the girl dug into their redoubt. In the next instant they saw it was over. The Trailsman had them dead in his sights. They drew rein, throwing down their guns, their arms lifted.

"All right, mister." Dutch Stacey snarled the words, his face twisted in pain, holding his shattered arm as he sat his horse, glaring at Fargo. "I'll be seeing you again."

"Not unless you're damned unlucky," Fargo said mildly. But that mild tone was set in steel. "Now get your ass out of here. You're lucky I didn't get mad at you." The round barrel of the Sharps swept the group. "You can leave your guns."

They were gone in a moment. Fargo waited, listening, to be sure. Then he whistled for the Ovaro.

"I suppose I should thank you," the girl said stiffly as she stood up and stepped out of the log fort. "I didn't realize you weren't one of them."

"The pleasure was mine," Fargo answered, a smile touching his lips as she took a step and began to limp.

"Though from your behavior I don't see that you're really all that different," she shot at him.

"I'm worse," he shot back at her, and reached out his hand to help her.

"Just don't touch me."

"Not until you ask me—nicely." And he swept her angry face with a big grin.

She had pulled her torn shirt around her, yet her

firm, springy breasts all but refused to be hidden to her great irritation as she began pulling and tucking to cover herself.

"You can ride back with me to the wagons."

"I'd rather walk!" she slashed at him.

"Suit yourself." He swung up onto the Ovaro, started to cross the clearing. Looking back, he watched her limping, her face set in determination. "Get up behind and sit on the saddle skirt," he told her, turning the horse.

"No, thank you!"

He kneed the Ovaro and in a moment had grabbed her arm. "Get up like I say or I'll put you up the way I had you before." He looked straight down into glaring hazel eyes. "Take my hand and then pull yourself up and over. It's easy."

She hesitated, tried another painful step, and said, "I suppose I have to, dammit!"

"We'll be moving fast; you better hold on to me."

"I'll see if I have to."

He grinned at the disgust she put into her voice as she settled herself on the saddle skirt behind the high cantle. "You'll have to, honey."

"Then the pleasure will be all yours."

Fargo's grin broadened. "Say, that's one for you."

In a few moments they reached the wagons. There was no sign of Stacey and his companions. The girls were standing around Kite Johnson, waiting to see what had happened.

"Thank God you're all right." Kite Johnson helped the girl down from the pinto, then offered his hand to Fargo. "I could use a drink. How about yourself?"

"Good enough. I'll take some water." The girls eyed the broad shoulders and big chest in open admiration as he loosened the pinto's cinch, slipped the bit out of his mouth.

"Mister, you wouldn't be heading for Washing Springs, would you?"

"I might be, honey." Fargo grinned at the short, green-eyed blond with the large pillowy bosom and sparkling mouth.

"My name's Frannie." Her frank eyes looked at him with a childlike friendliness.

"Glad to meet you, Frannie."

"I'm Kite Johnson," the wiry entrepreneur said, cutting in. "It'd be real good if you rode on in with us. It ain't far to the Springs, but those boys might take it in mind to come back."

Fargo was looking at the girl, who had moved toward Frannie and was testing her weight on her injured ankle.

"Sally, you all right?" the blond asked.

"I'm all right. I think it just twisted. Nothing broken. It'll be all right."

"You don't know how lucky you are. It would have been awful with those ugly men."

"I don't think I had much choice." Her tone was sour.

Fargo's grin spread across his face. "I like your way with the humor," he said.

The girl looked at him and said nothing.

"Say, you didn't tell us your name," Frannie said.

"That's right, I didn't."

"Well, what is it?" she prodded, laughing, and swayed slightly in his direction.

He could feel the heat coming from her and his own desire suddenly rising.

"Fargo," he said, "Skye Fargo." And at the words

he felt the girl Sally stiffen. The surprise was still in her face when he looked directly at her.

She regained her composure instantly. "I might have known." Her voice was soft, wry, almost as though she was speaking to herself. "Skye Fargo, the Trailsman."

"Something I can do for you, honey?"

"That depends."

"On what?"

"I've been looking for you."

The grin spread all over Fargo's face. "You dealt them, honey, now bet 'em."

JOIN THE <u>TRAILSMAN</u> READER'S PANEL
AND PREVIEW NEW BOOKS

If you're a reader of <u>TRAILSMAN</u>, New American Library wants to bring you more of the type of books you enjoy. For this reason we're asking you to join <u>TRAILSMAN</u> Reader's Panel, to preview new books, so we can learn more about your reading tastes.

Please fill out and mail today. Your comments are appreciated.

1. The title of the last paperback book I bought was: _____
_____

2. How many paperback books have you bought for yourself in the last six months?
☐ 1 to 3   ☐ 4 to 6   ☐ 10 to 20   ☐ 21 or more

3. What other paperback fiction have you read in the past six months? Please list titles:_____
_____
_____
_____

4. I usually buy my books at: (Check One or more)
☐ Book Store   ☐ Newsstand   ☐ Discount Store
☐ Supermarket   ☐ Drug Store   ☐ Department Store
☐ Other (Please specify)_____

5. I listen to radio regularly: (Check One)   ☐ Yes   ☐ No
My favorite station is:_____
I usually listen to radio (Circle One or more)   On way to work /
During the day / Coming home from work / In the evening

6. I read magazines regularly: (Check One) ·   ☐ Yes   ☐ No
My favorite magazine is:_____

7. I read a newspaper regularly: (Check One)   ☐ Yes   ☐ No
My favorite newspaper is:_____
My favorite section of the newspaper is:_____

For our records, we need this information from all our Reader's Panel Members.
NAME:_____
ADDRESS:_____ZIP_____
TELEPHONE: Area Code ( ) Number_____

8. (Check One)   ☐ Male   ☐ Female

9. Age (Check One)   ☐ 17 and under   ☐ 18 to 34
☐ 35 to 49   ☐ 50 to 64   ☐ 65 and over

10. Education (Check One)
☐ Now in high school   ☐ Graduated high school
☐ Now in college   ☐ Completed some college
☐ Graduated college

As our special thanks to all members of our Reader's Panel, we'll send a free gift of special interest to readers of <u>THE TRAILSMAN</u>.

Thank you. Please mail this in today.

NEW AMERICAN LIBRARY
PROMOTION DEPARTMENT
1633 BROADWAY
NEW YORK, NY 10019

Exciting Westerns by Jon Sharpe from SIGNET

		(0451)
☐ THE TRAILSMAN #1: SEVEN WAGONS WEST	(127293—$2.50)*
☐ THE TRAILSMAN #2: THE HANGING TRAIL	(110536—$2.25)
☐ THE TRAILSMAN #3: MOUNTAIN MAN KILL	(121007—$2.50)*
☐ THE TRAILSMAN #4: THE SUNDOWN SEARCHERS	(122003—$2.50)*
☐ THE TRAILSMAN #5: THE RIVER RAIDERS	(127188—$2.50)*
☐ THE TRAILSMAN #6: DAKOTA WILD	(119886—$2.50)*
☐ THE TRAILSMAN #7: WOLF COUNTRY	(123697—$2.50)
☐ THE TRAILSMAN #8: SIX-GUN DRIVE	(121724—$2.50)*
☐ THE TRAILSMAN #9: DEAD MAN'S SADDLE	(126629—$2.50)*
☐ THE TRAILSMAN #10: SLAVE HUNTER	(114655—$2.25)
☐ THE TRAILSMAN #11: MONTANA MAIDEN	(116321—$2.25)
☐ THE TRAILSMAN #12: CONDOR PASS	(118375—$2.50)*

*Prices slightly higher in Canada

Buy them at your local
bookstore or use coupon
on next page for ordering.